In *Hope of Heaven* John O'Hara has briefly taken off his brass knuckles to write a passionate and touching love story. But all the O'Hara elements are here. The toughness is here, and the bitter compassion, the tragic theme, disclosed with a chillingly casual, back-of-the-hand abruptness. And there are O'Hara's marvelous bystanders, charged with their habitual and desperate lusts, talking O'Hara's marvelous language, traveling their bewildered course from bookie to cocktail bar. And there are the O'Hara laughs, too—the ones that die in your throat.

Hope of Heaven is one of O'Hara's best books.

hope of heaven

by

john O'hara

 BANTAM BOOKS · NEW YORK

HOPE OF HEAVEN

A Bantam Book published by arrangement with
Random House, Inc.

PRINTING HISTORY

Harcourt Brace edition published March 1938
2nd printing March 1938

Included in "Here's O'Hara" published
by Duell, Sloan and Pearce, 1946

Bantam edition published January 1956

PRINTED IN THE UNITED STATES OF AMERICA
BANTAM BOOKS, 25 West 45th Street, New York 36, N. Y.

hope of heaven

MAYBE I am not the man to tell this story, but if I don't tell it no one else will, so here goes.

I was sitting in my office in the Studio one warm day last September. My feet were up on the desk, and I was admiring my new $35 shoes, and my $7.50 socks, and thinking how nice it would be to go out and get in my $2200 car and go for a ride. But that was out of the question. I was too far behind in my work, and they were beginning to turn on the heat. So I had to stay there and read the *Hollywood Reporter* and *Variety* and try to get my mind off the sound of the dynamo or the generator or whatever it was that made that sound. That sound never let up, and if you let yourself listen to it it had the effect of the dentist's drill, or the bastinado. That sound is in every studio that I've ever worked in, and I never have been able to determine just what it is. Some say it's a dynamo; some say it's the ventilating system; others say it's just water in the pipe-lines. Whatever it is, it's always near the writers' offices.

The door between my office and my secretary's was open, and I heard the phone ring. I looked up. My secretary.

"A Mr. Miller wants to speak to you," she said.

"What Mr. Miller?"

"A Mr. Don Miller—"

"What Mr. Don Miller? I know five Don Millers."

"If you'll give me a chance I'll tell you," she said.

"Are you still sore at me?"

"He says he's from Gibbsville. He says he's a friend of your brother's."

"Don Miller," I said. "He didn't say which brother he's a friend of?"

"No. I didn't ask him. He just said to tell you he was a friend of your brother's, and he came from your home town. That's Gibbsville, isn't it?"

"Right. Okay, put him on." I picked up the phone. "Hello."

"Mr. Malloy?"

"That's right."

"My name is Don Miller. I'm a friend of Pat, your brother?" There certainly was a question in his voice.

"Yes, I have one."

"Well, I wasn't sure. I mean, I wanted to be sure I had the right Malloy."

"Very common name," I said. "How *is* Pat?"

"Oh, he was fine the last I saw him. Uh—I don't exactly come from Gibbsville, Mr. Malloy."

"Oh, no?"

"No. I'm from Swedish Haven—"

"Well—four miles."

"That's right. Three and a half since they put the new road in. I guess you weren't home since they put the new road in."

"Nope. Two years since I've been home. How're things?"

"Oh, I guess all right. Uh—are you busy all day, Mr. Malloy?"

"Well, sort of," I said. Aw-haw, I thought; a touch.

"Well, how about tomorrow then? Are you busy tomorrow? I wanted to talk to you. I'm really a friend of Pat's, and I don't want to borrow any money, but I don't know anybody out here and I wanted some advice on something. I knew you were out here working, but I didn't know what studio till yesterday. I saw in the paper where you were working on some picture so I decided to call you."

"Well, I tell you," I said, "why don't you come around to the Studio around four o'clock. Do you know where it is?"

"Oh, sure."

"Okay. I'll leave word at the gate so they'll let you in, and if you have any trouble just have the cop phone me. Is that all right with you?"

"Oh, that'll be fine. Thank you very much. I'll be there promptly."

"See you then," I said, and hung up. "Miss *Wendell!*"

She appeared. "Yes?"

"Come here, dear?"

"Definitely no. Is that all you wanted?"

"It seems like quite a lot," I said.

"Well then, I'm going to lunch, *eef* you don't mind."

"Will you phone the gateman and tell him I'm expecting a Mr. Don Miller at four o'clock, and he's to let him in."

When I came back from lunch I busied myself for a while with Miss Wendell—Rose. It was no cigar; she was in one of her moods. I had kept her waiting an hour and a half in the Vine Street Derby the night before. She hated the Vine Street Derby because she said it was always full of Warner Brothers gangster types, and she had to wait alone. So I told her I was sorry, and then the story editor sent for me and when I finally got back to my office it was six-thirty and she had gone home. On my way out I remembered Miller and I asked the gateman if there had been a Mr. Don Miller to see me, and he said no; no one had asked for me since three o'clock, which was when this gateman went on duty. During the next few days I wondered about Miller, but I had other things on my mind. For one thing, the Studio let me go. They had decided to shelve the story I was working on, as they were unable to borrow Jean Arthur. So a month or so passed and I thought very little about Miller.

Then one night I was having dinner at a South Sea Island kind of restaurant, off Hollywood Boulevard. The girl with me was Peggy Henderson. Although she was only twenty-one or -two, Peggy and I were old friends. Sometimes I was in love with her, and sometimes she was in love with me; but never at the same time, as the saying goes. At this point neither of us was in love with the other. As a matter of fact she apparently was in love with a boy her own age, named Herbert, about whom she was very mysterious. For a long time she wouldn't introduce me to him or tell me anything about him, except that he was not in pictures and he was not a Californian. He was Jewish, she said.

"Well, that's hardly a novelty in your life," I said. "All your best friends are Jews. Except me."

"You're more Jewish than any Jew I know," she said.

I made her try to explain that, and she was explaining it when someone said: "Mr. Malloy?"

I looked up. "Yes."

"I'm Don Miller," he said.

"Oh, are you?" I said. I do not like strangers who introduce themselves when I am having dinner with a girl.

"Well, you don't have to get high-hat about it," he said.

"Oh, I'm not so sure," I said. "What do you want?"

"I only wanted to apologize for not keeping that engagement, but if you're gunna get high-hat, skip it."

"Oh, sit down," I said. "Miss Henderson, this is Mr. Miller. Will you have a drink?"

"No, thanks," he said. He bowed to Peggy. Nodded is a better word, although he kept looking at her. She looked at him the way she always looked at anyone new. She was always friendly, and she always studied new people.

"Have a drink, for Christ's sake. Don't sulk."

He smiled. "All right, thanks. I'll have a rye and soda."

"Mr. Miller is from my home town," I said.

"Gibbsville!" said Peggy.

"You're wonderful," I said. "He's a friend of my brother's. One of them. By the way, how did you know me? Don't tell me I look like Pat. Or don't tell Pat."

"No, nothing like that. Although I do see a family resemblance. No, I was sitting at the bar when you came in, and I heard the bartender call you Mr. Malloy, so I asked him if you were James Malloy. He didn't know, but the proprietor said yes, you were James Malloy."

"Mm. Well, what happened the other day?" I said.

"The other day? You mean a month ago? I called you since then but they said you weren't there any more."

"Well, that still doesn't answer my question," I said.

"Aw, I just couldn't get there that day."

"But why?"

"Why be so insistent, Jim? If he doesn't want to tell you," said Peggy.

"I'd rather tell you some other time," he said.

"All right," I said. "I suppose you don't need that advice any more?"

"Huh." He got a vague look in his eyes.

"Skip it," I said. "Drink up. Peggy?"

"I'm not ready for another one," she said.

"Waiter. A Tahitian Punch for Miss Henderson. A rye and soda for the gentleman, and I'll have a Scotch and soda."

Miller sat with us and got a little tight and insisted on buying some drinks. Presently Peggy excused herself and when she left the table Miller said: "Where can I get in touch with you?"

I was staying at an apartment hotel.

"Can I call you there tomorrow?" he said.

"Sure. But not before noon."

"Did you tell Pat you heard from me?"

"No," I said, "I never write home. Hardly ever. Why? Don't you want me to?"

"No. I wanta ask you a favor. Don't tell anybody you saw me."

Peggy came back to the table during the silence that followed his request, but I guess he understood that I would not tell anyone I had seen him, because right away he said: "Are you in the movies, Miss Henderson?"

"Oh, no. I work in a bookstore."

"Oh, you do? Where?"

"On Wilshire Boulevard."

"What's the name of it?"

"He's moving right in," I said.

Peggy laughed. "The Avon Bookshop. It's in Beverly Hills. Why, are you a great reader, Mr. Miller?"

"Me? I haven't read a book since Christ knows when," he said.

From then on he relaxed and we had a good evening.

2

THE MORNING after we saw Don Miller I drove Peggy to the bookstore. Peggy did not have a car. Her kid brother, who went to the University of California at Los Angeles, had an old jalopy; a Durant Six roadster. She seldom drove it, although she paid most of the bills for it. How she managed so well I never will know. Her mother was dead, and she had not seen her father in years. Once in a great while she would hear from him, from Mexico, Texas, Montana, South America, Chicago. Never from New York or Europe or the Orient. Looking at Peggy and Keith, her brother, and having known their mother, and knowing as much and as little as I did about her father's life, I had my own picture of what Mr. Henderson was like. From him I imagine Keith got his height and leanness and casual, contemptuous good looks. Peggy looked so much like pictures of her mother as a girl that there couldn't have been very much of her father in Peggy's appearance. About the only thing Peggy got from him, as far as I could make out, was her independence, of which she had a complete set. Once in a great while Peggy would get a letter, forwarded, addressed to a house in which she had not lived for four years. The letter would be from Mexico City, Houston, Missoula, Quito, Clark Street, and it would be written on hotel stationery or on the stationery of some club, and in it would be a money order for as little as fifty dollars or as much as five hundred. "Dear Kids—" it always began. I remember one time Peggy

showed me a letter from New Orleans and she asked me
what I thought he was doing. Well, it was hard to say.
Chicago and Missoula spoiled my theory that he was in
the oil business. The money order from New Orleans was
for five hundred, which led me to suspect that Henderson
might be mixed up in gun-running, because in that racket
they pay off good, and in gold, but I did not say so at
the time.

There was a peculiar reason why I did not say so. Aside
from not wanting to take away any of her pleasure at the
mere fact of getting five hundred dollars all at once, there
was a reason that would have been more important. Peggy
was politically almost as far left as she could go, and she
might have been afraid her father was running guns for
the wrong revolutionaries. There was nothing transitory
about her beliefs, and nothing new. Her conviction began
in high school; the things she learned in the intervening
years were really only additional information that made
for stronger conviction, until now she had become a sym-
bol to me. Whenever I read silly stuff about Reds I would
think of Peggy, and not of Mike Gold. Just as, whenever
I read silly stuff about Catholics I would think of my
mother and not of Cardinal O'Connell. Feeling that way,
it was a wonder Peggy and I did not get married, but it
might as well be understood this early that she had something to say about that. We can get that over with now,
so that it won't complicate things later.

On mornings like this, tooling my beautiful Buick out
to the bookstore, with the car working fine and Peggy
looking sweet and a good big breakfast inside us and the
morning air and a cigarette and the pretty jail-bait on
their way to high school and the sun and money in the
bank and no hangover—I would reach over with my right
hand and pull Peggy to me. (That was another good thing
about her: there was none of that "Somebody'll *see* us.")
"Do you love me?" I would say.

"No."

"Well, then, why don't you marry me?"

"I don't like you."

"Well, why don't you marry me? God damn it, we oughta get married. I think you do love me."

"What if I do! Suppose I did? I'd never marry you or anyone like you."

"We're friends, aren't we?"

"Yes, and that's all. Just because I *sleep* with you? Listen, we've had that out before—"

"Mm."

"Oh, now you're going to spoil it with your lousy puns and I'll be disagreeable at the shop. Why do you have to— why can't you just accept our relationship—and don't look hurt, and sulk. You know damn well, James Malloy, damn well you know it, if I said I would marry you you'd want to get out of it. If I said all right, you and I'll meet at two o'clock this afternoon and file intention to get married, I'll bet you'd be at the Vendome, drunk. Trying to get out of it."

"That's a lie, and you know it."

"It's the truth and *you* know it."

I always stopped the car about a block away from the bookstore. "All right. You're right. You're omniscient. You're Havelock Ellis. You're Dorothy Parker. You're Dorothy Thompson. You're Dorothy Dix. You're—whoever knows all about men and women and class-angling, and ideology, and human relations. Oh, you're so God damn smart. Why don't *you* face a fact or two? For instance, why don't you admit you're in love with this Herbert guy?"

"Because—why should I let you put words in my mouth? You object to my uh—omniscience. Well, I object to yours."

"All right, all right, all *right!*" I said.

"Major Bowes."

"That's corny," I said. "Well, then, listen, how about this? Suppose you don't love me. Suppose you don't even love this Herbert—"

"Why do you keep calling him this Herbert? Just call him Herbert. I'll get the idea. I'll know who you mean."

"Okay. Herbert. Suppose you don't love either one of

us, this me, or that Herbert. All right. Now, I don't know what goes on between you two, but I think I can guess."

"No, you can't."

"Yes, I can. And I'll surprise you. My guess is, you're not having an affair with Herbert. Right?"

"Well, yes. You're right. As far as you go you're right. But only as far as you go. Listen to me, Jim. For a so-called intelligent man you don't seem to realize one important thing about me. I don't say you give the matter much thought. I have a strong suspicion that when I'm not with you you don't give *me* much thought. But anyway, what you don't realize is, even if I'm not sleeping with Herbert, he's much closer to me than you are. Except when you are actually sleeping with me. Why *can't* you realize that? I like you. I do like you. And, I like to sleep with you. But you've made me so mad this morning I'm going to tell you something. I'd rather marry Herbert, and not sleep with anybody, than marry you."

"Mm," I said. "Well, that about finishes that." I looked straight ahead. I was hurt, because she never had said anything as strong as this. We had had substantially the same kind of discussion many times before, usually under approximately the same circumstances, but this was the first time she had been blunt. And I guess honest. I punched the steering wheel with both fists. It was a "safety" steering wheel that yielded a little to the punches, as it was supposed to yield to your body if you were in a collision. For a second I forgot her in my misery, and then I felt her looking at me. She reached over and put her hand on my knee.

"Hello," she said.

"Hello," I said.

"I'm sorry."

"No, you're not. You're sorry you made me feel this way, but you're not sorry you said what you did."

She did not deny this.

"Peggy. I have a feeling this isn't the time to bring this up, but I have one more proposition. You're the most realistic person I know. I don't mean that in any way but honestly. It isn't flattering, and it isn't unflattering. But you are. You're like Coolidge or somebody. I mean materialistic. Face facts. Good business head. That kind of thing. Well now, how about this? I would like to live with you. I have fun with you. I sort of love you. You have fun with me. You sort of love me. And even though we don't think the same way, or at least you think your way to things, for instance your leftist stuff, and I feel my way. But we arrive about the same place. Isn't that true?"

"More less."

"It is true. I haven't got a good thinking brain, but I have sound emotions. You can give me the party line on the Scottsboro boys or the Mooney case as though some God damn Jesuit worked it out for you. On the other hand, I know almost right away, without thinking, without using words like activize and ideology and dialectical materialism and all that crap, I am on the right side. That is, the leftist side. Isn't that true?"

"Yes, that's true."

"Well, what difference does it make how we get there as long as we get to the same place?"

"Oh, a lot of difference. Emotions aren't trustworthy."

"Did you ever hear of the false syllogism?"

"I don't depend on syllogisms."

I lit a cigarette. I put the lighter back into the socket on the dash. "Well, anyway. We've got so damn far away from my proposition. You concede most of what I say. You're realistic. I'm emotional. You like me. I like you. Now then. You concede these things?"

"Sure. Go on, or you'll get lost again."

"Well, why don't you marry me on this basis. I make a lot of money out here. You make twenty-two-fifty a week at the shop. You get an occasional pourboire from your old man, which you can't depend on. Keith keeps you broke, and probably when he gets out of college he'll get a job as filling-station attendant. Your grandfather—"

"Oh, we don't count on him."

"Well, you see what I mean. Marry me for my money. Marry me for economic independence. To do the things you want to do. As far as I'm concerned, it's a damn good bargain, so you don't have to worry about that angle." I turned and faced her. "Well, what do you think?"

"James. Dear James. I'll be late for work. I *am* late."

"Well, for Christ's sake, give me some kind of an answer, or at least comment. Don't be so God damn patronizing and superior. Dear James. Dear James. Dear James my ass."

She put out her finger and drew imaginary circles counter-clockwise on the crystal of the dash clock. "Uh, in the first place, you hate working for pictures, so as a realist I have to take that into consideration. How do I know you'll stick it out another year? Even one more year? I don't and you don't. So therefore I'd be taking that risk. In the second place, you said something about Keith. I'm not worried about Keith. He doesn't take much money. He practically earns his way through school. In fact, I'd say he does earn his way through. You know, he's a good athlete, and that's a great help. And then you mentioned something about my salary. Well, we don't live on my salary. We have some money from my mother's insurance. Enough to pay the rent and electricity and little debts, and the money I get from my father may not seem like much to you, but honestly, it does always come just when we seem to need it. I don't know why, but it just does. The little bluebird, or God, or something. And, one other thing besides. More or less covering the whole financial aspect. You talk about financial independence."

"Economic independence."

"Well—"

"No, not well. *Economic* sounds more like the kind of thing *you'd* say."

"Okay. But I wanted to tell you my theory. My theory is this. I haven't got the party line on it, Smartie, but it's this way. The only way, to secure economic independence, is to be independent of—is to be economically independent. In other words, I'll put it this way. It's a curious thing, but the more money you have, the less independent you are, is my theory. In other words, the very rich are the least independent of money, that is to say, independent of economic or financial problems. The very rich are just not economically or financially independent."

"Well, now, I don't know about that," I said. "As far as it goes it sounds all right, but I imagine it's specious or Utopian. I don't mean Utopian Sinclair Utopian."

"Ooh!" she said. "And you talk about corny."

"Right off the elbow. But we gotta have money. We gotta have wampum, or scrip. Kale. Mazuma. Spinach. Cabbage. Gelt. Uh—or amperes or volts or bushels. You know why paper money is? Or credit? Because it's too damn much trouble to be lugging gold all over the place—"

"Yes, I know, dear, and besides, there isn't that much gold. Yes, I know all that. Probably better than you do."

"That's right. Do you love me?"

"Yes, now I do. And I'll tell you something else that ought to make you feel better, or at least restore your masculine pride. Herbert has offered me almost the same proposition, and I've turned it down. Except that with Herbert there wouldn't be any sex. Herbert—now don't you ever repeat this—Herbert has T.B. A spot. He just loves me. And without working he has more money than I'll ever need. Does that make you feel better?"

"In a way, yes, in a way, no. Doesn't make any difference. You know what I'd like to do?"

"I think so. You want to go back to the hotel, or to my house. Is that it?"

"Yes. You take the day off. We'll go to the beach, or the hotel, or your place, or San Luis Obispo, or the desert or anywhere. Let's go on a trip?"

"I'd like to. Honestly I would. But I'm not going to marry you or Herbert or anybody, so I need my job. Now I have to go. I'm a worker."

"Arise, ye prisoners of starva-tion!"

"The first woman that comes in and wants to buy 'Gone with the Wind' I'm going to sell her 'The Coming Struggle for Power'—"

"Show her Strachey's picture."

"All right. I will."

"What if it's a man?"

"Men don't buy books in the morning," she said.

"Mm. And women don't buy enough of them."

"Right," she said. "Well, I have to go now. Oh, my."

"If you change your mind."

"I can't, Jim. I wish I could. What are you doing tonight, around ten o'clock?"

"No plans. Why?"

"I'm going to an anti-Fascist meeting. It ought to be over about nine-thirty. Do you want to meet me somewhere?"

We made the date and I sat in the car with my right arm stretched across the top of the seat. She was carrying her hat and she was wearing a sharkskin suit, not new, but one I liked. She always walked as though she were going some place. I liked her walk. I had nothing to do. When she turned the corner I got out of the car and went to a shop and bought some over-priced ties and then I went down Wilshire to Vine Street and Hollywood and bothered my agent, who had all the New York papers. I phoned the hotel and they said a Mr. Don Miller had called and left a number. I called him. He wanted to see me, so I said I'd take him to lunch, twelve-thirty.

3

I⊤ WAS a boring meal, up to the moment when Miller said he never drank coffee except in the morning.

He was there first, sitting on a tube-and-leather chair in the front of the restaurant, which was one of those modern eating places, all tin foil and black cloth and marble. He stood up. He was wearing an inexpensive Glen plaid jacket, cheap gray flannel slacks, imitation suède shoes, a dark brown polo shirt, and the conventional Hollywood neckerchief. His hair was cut short, but not "crew cut," and he was taller than he had seemed before. Everything about him seemed newer than his sunburn, and he was a very handsome young man.

It was a very boring meal, because his attitude seemed to say: "All right, get it up. Say something. Start the conversation. What have you got to say for yourself?"—which was not quite the case. After all, he had called me, not I him. Several times, during silences, I wanted to say the hell with it and get up and leave. There were at least two hundred other people in Hollywood I'd rather have lunched with.

He was a good six feet tall, with the kind of athletic build that is athletic, but one look at his face and you knew that this was no athlete. Probably he could do hand-stands on a beach. Possibly he could dive well. Maybe he had played high school basketball or had picked up some golf or tennis. He undoubtedly was strong, but in a way that I was not afraid of. He had long fingers, with long wide nails that had been buffed

15

to a nice shine. I bet myself that he played the piano, a
sort of fraternity-house piano; competent, unimaginative
piano; improvising-sounding, but someone else's impro-
visation. I could all but hear him, playing something like
"Easy To Love," which at that time was brand new. Slow,
not in any steady tempo, and all chords. That's what
those hands were for—at least that was one of the reasons
and explanations for them. I also could easily imagine
them going to work on a girl. It is not often that I notice
a man's hands, but I had to notice his, because by the
time his steak arrived I had taken a thorough dislike to
him, and that was the reason why I sized him up so carefully. It is often a good thing to look a man over carefully when you start out with such an active dislike of
him, and all during the meal I had a far-off notion that a
casual word, or a spilt glass of water might have us swing-
ing at each other. Well, I kept telling myself, this was
one decision I was pretty sure I could get.

We talked about what we were going to eat, and then
what we were eating, and about a couple of dolls who sat
across the room and the doll situation in Hollywood.
There was no specific talk; it was all general, even when
we talked about the food. I mean he didn't say his steak
was good or bad; he said it was funny how in California
the highest praise you could bestow on a steak was to say
that it was "New York Cut." "Yeah, that is funny," I said.
After a while the conversation settled down to a tempo:
three or four mouthfuls of food, and some remark about
movie extras and how some of them were easy to sleep
with and some of them were difficult. Neither of us took
dessert. One large coffee for me.

He didn't like my Luckies. He had Camels, which he
took out of his shirt pocket. He reached in, surrounded
the pack with his hand, slapped two fingers of his left
hand on the top of the pack (noisily, and much harder
than was necessary) until two cigarettes popped up. He
extracted one and put it in his mouth. He scratched a
match and held it to the cigarette and cocked his head
far over to one side and took a deep inhale. Enough smoke

to fill a bicycle tire came out of his mouth and he blew
out the match. Whenever you see a man go through all
this you are looking at a man who has had plenty of time
on his hands.

I could hardly look at him. I decided to shock him.

"What's on your mind, Miller?"

Some of his cockiness went away and he took another
quick drag on his cigarette. He looked down at the cigarette, which he was rubbing against the ash tray. "Plenty,"
he said. "But I don't know—I'll be frank with you. I don't
know if I want to talk about it."

"You mean to me or just to anybody?"

"Anybody, I guess. Yes, anybody. I might as well tell
you this. No, God damn it, I don't know what the hell.
Jesus, I don't know anything. God damn it."

I waited. I watched him crush the cigarette.

"You don't like me, do you?" he said.

"I don't know," I said. "Why? What makes you think
that?"

"You gave me that impression. I guess you think I'm
a fresh guy. Well, I am. I always was, I guess."

I waited again.

"You know, I used to know you," he said.

"Did you? When?"

"Remember when you used to come down to Swedish
Haven and write up the football games? You were
working on the *Leader*."

"I remember, yes."

"You wrote me up in a game and you spelt my name
wrong. The only time you ever wrote me up."

"Miller? For Christ's sake, how could I spell that
wrong?"

"It's not my name."

"Oh," I said. "Oh-h-h." Three notes. "What is your
name?"

"That's the God damn trouble."

"You mean you don't want to tell me?"

"I don't want to tell anybody. Do you know anything about me? I mean, did you hear anything from Pat, today? This morning?"

"Nope. I'm not even sure Pat can write."

"Pat's all right. He used to be a good friend of mine. He's a good guy. We used to go out and get cockeyed together."

"You know, if you don't like Pat you don't have to say you do. I don't like him, so don't let that worry you. What's the matter? Are the cops looking for you, or what?"

"Mr. Malloy, I'll lay my cards on the table. Do you remember the Reverend Schumacher?"

"Sure. Pastor of the uh, Lutheran Church?"

"Reformed. That's the one. That's my father. He's dead, but that's the one you mean."

"A bald-headed man, a little heavy, about medium height. He was a Phi Beta Kappa."

"That's the one."

"Sure, I knew him. I liked him. I didn't know him very well, but I remember he wasn't a Kluxer. I think he was a patient of my father's at one time." I could see he wasn't listening much to this. Another silence.

"Some fresh coffee, sir?"

"Yes, I'll have some. Do you want a drink? One of your rye and sodas?" I said.

"No. No, thanks."

"Just some more coffee," I said. I lit a cigarette. "Well, listen, Schumacher—by the way, how did I spell your name?"

"S, h, u, m, a, c, h, e, r."

"That was a typographical error. I knew how to spell your old man's name, so I'd know how to spell yours. Anyway, you're in some kind of a jam, and you have some idea I can help you. That's right so far, isn't it?"

"Yes. I'm in a jam. I don't know why I phoned you in the first place. I had to talk to somebody, then when the time came, like the time I was to come to your office over in the Studio, I couldn't make myself go over. It's the same way now. I phoned you today because I wanted to talk about it."

"What kind of a jam is it? Money? A dame?"

"Well—money. Oh, what the hell, I might as well tell you."

"Whenever you're ready. I don't have to tell you I won't repeat it."

"Oh, that don't worry me." He smiled. "You know something? I remember one time Pokey Armbruster, when he was coaching S. H. High, he was worried the night before the Gibbsville High game, because he remembered how you knew all our plays, and your brother Pat was playing on Gibbsville High. Remember that one play from a place kick formation where the guy holding the ball—"

"Sure. It was an old Lafayette play."

"Well, that was the one we beat Gibbsville on. So from then on, when Pokey realized how you didn't tell them the play, we all trusted you. Not that *I* ever had anything to trust you with, but all the same."

I let him talk on, because some of my antagonism was disappearing. He was letting himself go and was becoming a frightened kid who had to talk to somebody.

"It seems funny, sitting here in Hollywood, talking about S. H. High and all that stuff." He lit another cigarette, but not with all the motions he had gone through with the other. He took a sip of water, and a quick look at me. He watched the waiter pour my coffee, and when the waiter had gone he began: "When my old man died, for a while I lived with my aunt in Swedish Haven. She was my mother's sister and she was a strict old maid, so when I'd come in late at night she'd bawl me out the next morning, also because I didn't have a job. The only money I had was from my old man's lodge insurance, about enough to pay for the funeral and a little over. I had a Ford coop and I used to go around with the fellas and sometimes lend the car out for a couple dollars, and when we'd go out on a double date I'd supply the car and

the other fella'd buy the gas and I had a girl, she was
stenographer for old Mossbacher, at the shirt factory,
and he kept her. Old Mossbacher, he must be sixty-some
years old, but I don't know. She'd never tell me much
about him, but she was always good for ten bucks a week
and a couple times we took trips. She used to get sore
when I razzed her about Mossie. I used to say to her,
'Don't tell me old Mossie gives you the works.' And she'd
get sore.

"Well, so anyway I was just about breaking even. I
played a pretty good game of pool and I put up a good
appearance because I had these clothes I bought when I
was at State. I went to State for a year and a half after I
got out of High, but I flunked out. I don't know. I got so
I didn't give a God damn. So I used to pick up a couple
bucks shilling at Jimmy's poolroom. That's new since you
were there. But after a while the whole thing got on my
nerves. I used to look at these muggs that used to come in
the poolroom and I used to think, 'What the hell am I
doing wasting my time with them?' Their idea of something hot was to be a brakeman on the railroad and have
a regular run. They used to drive me nuts. And this dame
got on my nerves. I felt sorry for her in a way, but I wasn't
responsible. Mossie'd keep her at the office after everybody went home and after he went home she'd call me up
at my aunt's place and my aunt knew who she was and
she'd raise hell. Those old maids, you know they always
know when there's something funny going on. I had a
friend of mine had a dose and my aunt, I swear she knew
he had it before I did, even if I did see him every day.
And this kid I was traveling around with, my aunt used
to raise hell about her, and the kid, she'd call me up after
Mossie'd leave. She'd have to see me right away. So I'd go
over and pick her up and she'd make me drive right out
the Valley, without any supper, and I'd give her a jump in
the car. Well, that part of it was all right, but I began to
get worried. You know, I used to kid her about Mossie,
about these times when he'd been at her. I remember in

Psychology reading about some of these old guys and I thought it was a lot of crap. Oh, I'm no kid. But this stuff I used to read, I used to think those old English colonels and Chinks—but not Americans. Not old Mossie. You know, guys with whips or pushing pigeon's eyes out. This kid used to be nuts, absolutely screwy after he got through with her. She earned her pay, all right. Anyway, I got worried, because she'd cry and she was the hottest little babe I ever knew and I had some premonition I was getting into something. You know. Maybe she'd commit suicide, or Mossie'd do something to her and she'd die. And Mossie knew about her laying me. I'd see him on the street and he'd look at me with this dirty look in his eye and say, 'Good *eve*-ning, Harold, good *eve*-ning,' and give me a sort of, you know. Look. So I thought it was about time I got the hell out of there.

"There were no jobs, of course. It was all right with my aunt if I loafed around the poolroom all day and wasted my time, but take a WPA job or something like that? Oh, no. We were too good for that. I had to get out of town, so I went to a fella that knew Asa Merritt, the Congressman, and I got a letter to Merritt and I went to Washington. I sold my car and my aunt gave me fifty bucks and I went to Washington. I knew a guy there, he was a Beta, which I was and he flunked out the same time I did. I stayed with him. His parents were over in Europe.

"Well, it took me a couple days to get to see Merritt and he stalled me but he said he knew my old man and since I was in Washington anyway, I should stick around and maybe he could find something for me.

"Well, one afternoon I was walking along F Street and I kicked this thing, I thought it was a wallet. It looked like a wallet, and I picked it up and then I thought it was a checkbook. But do you know what it was? It was a book of these traveler's checks. A whole book of them, not one of them torn out. Brand new. I stuck the damn thing in my pocket, thinking sort of in the back of my head that I'd turn it in at some bank and probly get a reward for it.

You know why? Because it was for five thousand dollars. Five G's. There were ten checks, each made out for five hundred dollars. A lot of money, you know.

"So the next day I had to go see Merritt, and this time the son of a bitch finally got around to telling me the truth. He said, 'Harold, I'm very sorry to tell you, but I can't seem to be able to find anything for you.' He was polite and all like that, because he probly was afraid he was losing a vote, and you know, like what if I went back home and said Congressman Merritt was high-hat? It might hurt him politically. But irregardless he didn't have any job for me.

"That was one thing. Then when I went home that day, late in the afternoon, back to this guy's apartment that I was staying at, Joe said to me, he told me his mother and father were coming back from Europe the following Monday and he had to go to New York to meet them and I'd have to get out of the apartment. We had to get a colored fella to clean the place up after the way we left it. Joe said why not go to New York with him, maybe I could find a job there. Fat chance, I thought, and anyway I didn't have more than about ten bucks and being stuck in New York on ten bucks.

"Swell luck I was having all of a sudden. Then I got this idea. I remembered about this book of traveler's checks. I didn't say anything to Joe about it, but I told him I'd let him know the next day in regard to New York.

"I went to my room and I got out this book of checks and I looked at it and looked at it. I never saw one before, so I studied it carefully and the idea came to me, when I was a kid I used to be able to sign my old man's name to excuses when I bagged school. I was pretty good at it. Right now I could sign the old man's name and if you knew his signature you'd think it was all right. So I sat down at a desk and I began writing out, Donald R. Miller, Donald R. Miller, copying it over and over again, oh, a couple hundred times. This checkbook was in the name of Donald R. Miller, and there was his signature right there in the book, ten times, so I studied it, the different ways he wrote it himself, and by the time I went to bed that night I could write Donald R. Miller better than my own name.

"Well, to make a long story short, I went to New York with Joe, my friend, only I went to a different hotel, a better one, and I told Joe I was registering under the name of Donald R. Miller. I gave him some phony reason like I was afraid I'd run into somebody or something. I put up a good front. I had these clothes and a couple good suitcases and I looked the part. I even went out and called up the hotel and left messages for myself. Please call Mr. Gump at the University Club. Call So and So at the Bankers Trust Company. Mrs. J. Archibald Smith would like you to come to dinner Thursday. Every day I'd have a lot of messages. Maybe the clerks didn't read them, but maybe they did. And I was there about three days and I got dressed up every night and when I'd go out I'd say to the clerk, if there were any messages for me I'd be at such and such a number, and then I'd go right out and call myself up. I had those guys thinking I was the most important guy in New York. They probly thought I was some rich man's son from Washington, D.C. I registered from Washington.

"Well, the third day, or rather night, I got all duked up and went out and ate a sandwich at some joint over on Third Avenue and went to a movie till around ha' past eleven and then I came back and I asked the clerk, I said I wanted to cash a traveler's check. I said it was pretty big and he didn't have to give me all the money all at once. I only wanted fifty bucks, I told him. So that made it look all right and he gave me a hundred. I signed that thing, boy, every minute I expected to have some cop thump me on the shoulder, but I guess they probly compared my signature with the one on the register and it looked the same. They had three signatures. The one when I registered, the one on the check, and the one I signed right then when I cashed the check.

"They gave me the rest of the dough the next day and I stayed there the rest of the week. I even gave a party

right there in the hotel when Joe's mother and father
came back. We got two nice babes, respectable, and the
party set me back around seventy dollars. Joe sort of
wondered, but I let him guess. Jesus, Malloy, I'm giving
you all the chance in the world to get me thrown in the
clink."

"Sure you are," I said.

"Well, I'm taking that chance."

"You certainly are."

"I guess if I tried to move in on your girl you wouldn't
let me get very far."

"Well, then, don't try," I said. "But go on with your
story. Didn't they ever catch up with you?"

"Never did. It was a funny thing. To get money I had
to spend money. I went out and bought a new outfit, new
bags, packed up, took a taxi to the Penn Station, checked
the bags, came back a while later and got them, and
registered at another hotel. I stayed at two hotels at the
same time. I used the cash I got from one hotel to set me
up at the second one, and then I cashed another check at
the second hotel. In about two weeks' time I had over a
thousand bucks cash, so I decided it was time to blow. All
this time I was expecting some flatfoot to be waiting for
me, but I got so I didn't care. I was living the way I
always wanted to. There was a little dame at the place
where they sold tickets to the shows, in the hotel. I'd go
there and buy two tickets to a show and only use one. She
got to know me, so I took her out and laid her, and
through her I got to know some others. She was all right,
too, this ticket girl. Oh, I did another little thing, just to
make it all look on the up and up. I'd call Joe in Washington every couple days, just in case they checked up on
the bill, I'd have these Washington calls. I was wishing I
could have stayed there till I spent the whole five grand,
but I had other plans. I wanted to get the cash and blow,
which I did. When I was sure of having a thousand bucks
all clear, and my bills paid, I checked out of the two hotels
and I came out here.

"I been out here ever since. This place reminds me of

those Western stories I used to read, where they don't ask you your name or where you came from or anything. I'm as much Donald Miller as I am anybody. I have a car and a license in the name of Miller, and for a laugh, I even told them at this place where I'm living, I said I was trying to get in the movies under the name of Don Mills, but my real name was Miller, but if any calls came for Don Mills, that was me. Oh, I've had a lot of laughs."

"But still you're worried. Why?"

"Wouldn't you be? What if they begin catching up with me? I can't understand why they haven't. This Miller guy, he must of been a crook or something, or else why doesn't he report losing five thousand bucks? That's the only answer I can think of. He must of been a crook." He took out a cigarette but did not light it. He held it in his thumbs and forefingers, fingering it as though he were rolling a cigarette. "Anyhow, it'd make a good story for you, wouldn't it?"

"I'd like to know the ending of it," I said.

"*You* would? What about *me*?"

"Uh, to get back to why you're telling me all this, you said you were in a jam. What kind of a jam? I mean, is it anything new besides your, uh, criminal record? You know, these banks and insurance companies are tough. If they ever do catch up with you they'll put you in that jail-house and throw the key away. My advice is, if you care anything about it, my advice is to be satisfied with what dough you have and try to get a legitimate job, under your real name. You could buy in on a hot dog stand or something like that."

"Me run a hot dog stand after the way I've lived! Say, that's the God damn trouble. Supposing I did buy a hot dog stand and went honest? Supposing I made enough dough to pay them back? That's just when they would catch up with me. Just when I was going honest. No, the hell with that. I considered going under my real name, but this hot dog stand idea stinks."

"Anyway, you're not in any immediate jam, other than what you've been in the past six months or so?"

"No."

"Then what are your plans? What's it all about? Why did you tell me all this?"

"Well, I had to tell you. I had to tell somebody. It may sound as if I was bragging, and I guess maybe I was, but I been thinking, I got away with this so far, why not use my brains to get into something honest, but where there was a lot of dough."

"Oh, I guess that's where I come in. Do you want to be a writer?"

"Don't kid me. Me write? Listen, when I write Donald R. Miller on a check or anything else."

"You're certainly one of the highest-paid writers I know."

"No, that writing, that's not for me. I haven't a big enough of a vocabulary, and I'm a lousy speller. No, what I want is some job that pays a good salary and I don't have to work too hard or get dirty. And I don't want to start from the bottom."

"It's too bad you're not a writer," I said. "Well, I'm sure I don't know what the hell I can do for you. Right now I'm not working myself. You have no ideas about what you want to do? No special training or anything like that?"

"Huh. If you call playing a good game of pool, or I can drive a car better than most guys. I'm a good dancer and I have plenty of clothes."

"You'd make a good dress extra. You know what that is?"

"One of those guys that has a full dress, long tails? Sure, I know about them. There's a couple of them living where I live. You can have that. No, I want a real job. I bet I could sell. Real estate, or cars. Cars I'd be good at. Good cars, like say a Packard or Duesenberg."

"How old are you?"

"You want to know the truth?"

"Mm."

"I'm twenty-two. I look older. I could pass for twenty-seven." He made a fist and punched the palm of his left hand. "Oh, Christ, Malloy, I don't know what I am, or anything. Here I started out to tell you about myself, and you listened, and I didn't tell you the truth. Not all of it. I left out some, and put in some. I'm gettin' so I don't know what's the truth and what isn't. I wasn't cut out for this stuff I'm doing. I'm no crook. I should of been a rich guy instead of a minister's son without any dough. I can fool people into thinking I'm rich, and all I need is a few bucks and clothes. I just sit around and look wise. When I'm doing it I get a great laugh out of it at the time, like with those checks, but when I'm alone, God, I don't want to go to jail. All I want is a good job and then I'd even pay back the money, providing I was sure I wouldn't get caught. When I used to make a living playing pool I was always honest. Oh, I used to lose a couple games on purpose and then make the bets bigger, but that's business."

"That's what they call a loss-leader."

"Sure. But anyway, I am honest. I'd like to sell a car that I wouldn't have to be ashamed of, maybe get the better of a guy on a trade, but that's business." He took a deep breath.

"It's after three," I said. "Give me your phone number and if I hear of anything I'll give you a buzz. Where do you live?" He gave me the address and phone number, and I paid the bill. He stood up, and by that act alone he changed. He was cocky again.

"Well, thanks for the lunch, old man. Gimme a buzz." He almost looked around to see if anyone was admiring him.

"Oke," I said, and he left me.

4

THE HENDERSONS lived in a little one-story house in the general direction of the Observatory. It took at least half a dozen visits before you knew the way, because of the winding roads and the names of the roads. They would take a name, say, Orchard, and there would be Orchard Road, Orchard Lane, Orchard Place, Orchard Drive, all together, intersecting and merging. It took a lot out of you to get there, too, because they have changed the ratios of steering-gears so you have to whirl your wheel continually all the way up to the Hendersons'.

I had the privilege of walking in without ringing the doorbell, and anyway I wore leather soles, which could be heard on the short cement walk and the wooden porch.

"Anybody home? Oh, hello, Keith."

"Hello, Jim."

"Don't get up," I said. "Sit still."

"Peggy isn't home yet." He was stretched out on a davenport. He rested his book, a fat textbook, on his belly. "What's new?"

"Nothing much."

He sucked his teeth, a habit of his. "Want a piece of pie? Millie baked a darn good pie tonight. Sweet potato pie."

"No, thanks, I just had dinner and a couple of drinks."

"I can get you a drink. Scotch? I think we have some Scotch."

"No, thanks. How're things out at Westwood?"

"Oh, 'bout the same as usual."

"Gonna make Phi Bete?"

"Me? Not a chance. Well, maybe. Accidentally. I won't try for it. I'm not altogether convinced of the, uh, uh, value of Phi Bete. I'm not so sure about it. There was a fellow in my fraternity last year, now he should have been Phi Bete. He was one of the most brilliant fellows I ever knew, really brilliant. Some of the nitwits that did make it, cats! They couldn't carry his books, this fellow. They weren't in the same league with him. But, he had some trouble with I don't know, English prof, or French. French I think. And, he just didn't get Phi Bete. Cats! I dunno." He rubbed the back of his head, fast and like a groom curry-combing a horse. "Do you think it's worth-while?"

"In a way. A negative way. If you make it, if you have a key, then you can throw it away in the bureau drawer and forget about it. If you haven't got it and you pan it, then people naturally think you're sour-grapes. I guess that's about all it's worth. Get it and forget about it."

"Guess you're right. You've got something there. Yep. But I'm not going to try for it. If I get it, okey-doke. If I don't, well. What are you working on? Haven't seen you around for a while."

"I'm working on my agent right now. Otherwise, nothing. They aren't doing that picture I was working on, so I'm looking for another job."

"I guess you won't starve. I don't know what's keeping Peggy. Did you have a date with her?"

"She's at a meeting. Yeah, I had a date, but you never know about those meetings."

"Do you think that's a good idea, those meetings? I'm against Fascism. My God. But what do you think of those meetings? I don't mean for Peggy now, but just generally speaking."

"Oh, they don't do any harm. It's better than nothing. At least it shows the Fascists that we know they're having *their* meetings, and then also if it weren't for the meetings a lot of people would just forget about the whole thing."

"That's true. Um-hm. True. I went to two of them with
Peggy, but, cats! I don't know, Jim. Same kind of people
get up and do the speechmaking there as at school. I mean
the same type. Cheerleaders. What if there hadn't been a
depression. I wonder if Peggy'd be going to anti-Fascist
meetings. Or if there'd be any meetings at all. I'm too
young I guess. I don't know enough, and all I learn is
what they teach me. I'll grow up, I guess."

"You'll be all right, Keith. You're all right now. You
can't have all the answers at your age. You can't at any
age, no matter how long you live, so don't let it worry
you. That's the difference between you and me. One of
them. When I was about your age I thought I knew all
the answers, but *you* know you *don't*. I guess this is Peggy.
I wonder who's with her."

"Hello. Hello, brother darling."

"Peggy. Hello, Herbert."

"Hello, Keith. Good evening, Mr. Malloy."

"Hello," I said. This spoiled my plans.

"James, I brought Herbert along because I knew you'd
have your car and I, Herbert has to go downtown and he'd
have to take a bus. We can all go together, except Keith.
You study."

"I don't want to go," said Keith. "Or, maybe I do. I'll
have to give the matter a little more mature consideration. Do I want to drive downtown, or don't I? What
advantage is there to be gained? No novelty in it. I've
been there. Charming company. True. But is it worth—"

"While he's giving the matter his mature consideration
let's go. Let us know when we get back," said Peggy. "By
the way, don't take that seriously, little man. I mean, don't
wait up for us."

"Little man. Lit-tle—man, eh?" Keith was more than six
feet tall, and built on the lines we have been led to believe
Lincoln's were. He very deliberately placed his book upon
the table and very deliberately rose.

"Don't you dare! Don't you touch me," said Peggy.

"Lit-tle man. Lit-tle man," he repeated. He suddenly
changed his posture and manner. He bent forward and

held out his arms like a bear or an ape, and let out a Tarzan yell. Peggy ran and we, Herbert and I, followed her.

The three of us sat in the front seat, Peggy in the middle. "Where to, Herbert?"

"The Los Angeles Biltmore," he said.

"See what's on the radio," said Peggy.

"There's something wrong with it," I said. I switched it on, but it was bad, mostly static. On the way we passed the house I had had the first time Peggy ever stayed with me. I looked down, and across my shoulder at her, but she was looking straight ahead. We were silent for blocks.

"Malloy, tell me, how much did you make out of your book. I mean, about how many copies did you sell?" said Herbert.

"Which one? There were two."

"The—the popular one. The one about the policeman in Central Park."

"Oh, thirty thousand copies, including the English sales. Figure about thirty cents a copy and you have the amount," I said. He annoyed me.

"Mm. Nine thousand dollars. Imagine, a book of that kind making nine thousand. How long'd it take you to write it?"

"You mean in work-hours, or over how long a period of time on the calendar? And why? Are you writing one?"

"Oh, I've written several. Unpublished. I can't publish while I'm living off my family."

"What kind of books do you write?"

"Well, one is an epic poem, something like 'Buddenbrooks,' by Thomas Mann. You know Thomas Mann."

"Not personally. Do you?"

"No. But I know his work very well. In German."

"Are you, uh, writing this, uh, epic poem in German? I thought 'Buddenbrooks' was prose."

"Oh, it is. Of course. No, you see mine is *like* 'Buddenbrooks,' a book about a family, you *know*?"

"Yes. Family. *I* know."

"But mine's American. Jewish-American."

"I see. The last time I talked to you you were doing something for two pianos."

"Herbert doesn't play any more," said Peggy.

"I've given up the piano, permanently. It takes too much out of me. I'm not good enough at it, and the effect of even good piano is too ephemeral. De Pachmann dies, where is his art? Lost. Lost until one of these radio geniuses can recapture sound floating through the ether. You've heard of that, how they're going to be able to tune in and get the Gettysburg Address and the Sermon on the Mount. What kind of a voice do you suppose Jesus Christ had, Peggy?"

"Beautiful, I'll bet."

"Anyway soothing," I said.

"Soothing? Soothing I'm sure is precisely the word. Soothing. Soft. Not exactly musical. Mildly hypnotic. The kind that the Hindu fakirs have when they induce mass hypnotism."

"You sound a little as if you had something against him," I said.

"Oh, shut up," said Peggy.

"All right," I said.

"No, don't," said Herbert. "I want to find out about books, from an author. You see, Malloy, I'm writing a novel about Los Angeles, present-day Los Angeles. The Angelus Temple. This fellow that killed his wife with the box of rattlesnakes. The Neon signs. The health people. No movie stuff. I'm going to ignore the movies."

"Who's your principal character? The fellow with the rattlesnakes?"

"No. In fact I may not even use him at all, but this town is full of people like him. It's a fantastic place, you know, Malloy. Fantastic. You know why? Because it's so incredibly ordinary."

"Mm."

"Fantastic. It's in a semi-tropical climate. It has a Spanish name, with religious Roman Catholic connotations. A rather large Mexican population and Oriental. The architecture, that is, I mean by that the Monterey house and the Mission stuff, is Mexican and Spanish and a little Moorish. And yet, Malloy, consider this: the really fantastic thing about it is that it's the crystallization of the ordinary, cheap ordinary American. The people. The politics. The cults. These Iowa people that come here and really assert themselves. They do what they wanted to do in Iowa but couldn't, for various and sundry reasons. The crazy clothes they all wanted to wear back in Iowa. And of course it's no city, except in population. Fantastically ordinary, cheap, commonplace. And I'm going to put it in a book, which is the reason why I've been plying you with questions about your books. I want my book to be a success, and I want to know what constitutes a successful book. Not a succes d'estime, but a financial success."

"Any book that makes any money is a financial success. From the author's point of view, any book that makes more than the two-fifty or five-hundred advance royalty."

"Well, of course I want mine to do better than that. Thank you very much, Mr. Malloy. I'm going to buy a car next week, and I hope I can repay this. Peggy, au 'voir. I had a pleasant evening. Thank you for my dinner. Now I go to face one of my capitalistic uncles, the bastard. Goodnight."

"Your heart's not in it, but as long as your body is I guess I have no kick coming."

"It's a nice body, so I'm told," said Peggy.

"Who told you?"

"You did," she said. "Light one for me, will you, please?" She took the cigarette but put it out after a few puffs. She was not what you would call an ardent smoker. She dinched it in the ash tray and then she settled back, apparently getting herself comfortable for a lengthy contemplation of the ceiling; but in a little while she took her hands from in back of her neck and lay over on her side and put her left arm across my chest. "I may marry you after all," she said, into the corner of the pillow.

"Oh, no. Not me."

"Yes, you," she said.

"Although it's as good an offer as I've had today."

"What is that? That's the last line of a dirty joke, isn't it?" She raised her head a little, angrily.

"I think so. But I don't know the joke."

"I'm glad, because—oh, Jim. I'm depressed, depressed. Why don't I tell Herbert to go away or leave me alone? Why do I feel so awful about the Jews under Hitler? Do you think Keith is a virgin?"

"Very likely."

"I wonder what he thinks about you and me," she said.

"He probably knows exactly where we are this minute. He's no dope. I've known about two kids like him in my life. They have an intelligence that transcends sex, or at least it keeps them out of that kind of trouble. Then, when the time comes, they get a girl, and the girl seems to be very well satisfied in that department. At least the other two guys I knew have wives that *look* very well taken care of, and content, and wouldn't cheat for anything. What about Herbert. Have you stayed with him yet?"

"Nope. I told you he has T.B. Put your arms around me. What are you thinking?"

"Nothing. I guess I may be in the middle of a train of thought. I have a theory that you're always thinking, always, always, always thinking. Isn't it awful? Think of being thinking all the time. Your brain banging away on all lobes."

"Well, that's what it's there for." She took a deep breath and gave it voice as she exhaled. "Hello."

"Hello."

"What's this?"

"Search me. I just happened to notice it there myself. Some kind of a growth, I imagine."

"Maybe you ought to see a doctor about it."

"I've seen enough doctors about *that*," I said. She lay on her back, I lay on my back, and she held my hand and we looked at the now dark white ceiling, and I don't know about her, but I had the illusion of walking hand in hand.

"This is nice, but I've got to go home tonight," she

said. "I think you're right about Keith. I think he does know you and I go to bed, but I have a theory about that. Keith's a funny boy. If I went to him and said, 'Keith, I'm having an affair with Jim Malloy,' he'd probably say he knew, and from then on everything would be easy. I mean, I could stay out all night any time I wanted to, and he wouldn't hold anything against you. But I don't want to do that. I don't want to come right out with it, because the kind of relationship you and I have, it may break off any minute. Any day. You might fall madly in love with someone, or I might, and right after I'd told Keith, and then I'd have to tell him the same thing about someone else. Then he'd think his little sister is a tart. Which she isn't."

"No. She isn't."

"And he's going through enough right now without any additional worries about me. He likes you."

"I like him."

"I must go now," she said.

"No."

"Yes."

"No. No, I said."

"Ah, Jim. Jimmy."

"That's right, my sweet."

5

THEN for a few weeks Peggy and I did not see each other, which meant that I did not see Keith or Herbert. Also I did not see Mr. Don Miller, but that did not seem like much of a loss. Don Miller was the kind of man that for the most part it is a fortunate thing not to have to make up your mind about. There are people whom you see and you react to in a certain way, a way unfavorable to them, from your own point of view. You see them, like at a party or a racetrack or on a train. You know them and you are on a first-name basis. Maybe you sit down and have a couple of drinks, talking about—well, just talking. If you ask this kind of acquaintance about a mutual acquaintance it invariably is a friend of *yours* whom he knows, and not a friend of *his* that you know. I don't know why this is so, because there are reasons why it should not be so. Maybe it is because in mentioning *your* friend, who knows him, you are subconsciously standing beside your friend, in a two-against-one alliance. You just plain don't like this Don Miller kind of guy, but the chances are about five to one that there never is an open break. You even give him credit for some good qualities, unimportant ones. I could and did readily concede, for instance, that Don Miller was a handsome young man. By the time this story was ended and I had seen him more frequently than I had at this point, I would have conceded that he dressed more like an Easterner than a Californian. I saw right away, the first time I met him on the Coast, that Miller was a guy who very probably could give me some trouble if we were both after the same girl. He also had a kind of courage that made him become Don Miller and stick to it. Under the same circumstances I would have been satisfied with the reward; or I might even have merely dropped the book of traveler's checks in a mailbox and let it go at that. The kind of courage that it takes to be a certain kind of phony is something I envy. In its way it's wonderful, the self-confidence of these guys. It's easy enough to go around being a jerk if your father happens to be President of the United States. But to make up your mind to be something, even if it is something you're not, and to be it, and to be successful at being it well, maybe Joan Crawford did want to hire a bross bond, but that's a long way from five shows a day at the Capitol, and she made it. I'll take Mike Romanoff, and you can have Brian Ahearn. (But the trouble with all this is that you can also take the Lunts, and I'll take George Burns and Gracie Allen.) So anyway —Don Miller.

As I say, for a few weeks I did not see Peggy and the others. I could have got seven-fifty at one studio, but my last job, my last four jobs, had been paying me a thousand. Not that seven-fifty is tin, but about this time they were getting ready to release an epic that I helped with, on which I was getting screen credit, and I knew the picture couldn't miss. That meant that as soon as the picture was released I would be getting a thousand again, somewhere. I was four or five thousand dollars ahead, and I hadn't been to New York for a year, so it was New York.

New York was wonderful. The wonderful dirty old Jersey meadows. The wonderful Pulaski Skyway. Beautiful Vesey Street and the dear sweet asafoetida warehouses. Bert Lahr doing his swing song in "The Show Is On." The shrunken-looking kids in tails, trying to show that Twenty-One was an old story to them—but walking directly to the kitchen when what they wanted was the men's room. Jack White and Pat Harrington, than whom, and Screwball and Jerry and Doctor R. E. Lee. Sherman Billingsley making his million and not losing anything by it. Charlie

Lucas, a good man to have on your side. My charming
pals among the Swing Street taxidrivers. My waiter
friends, Vincent and Karl and Georgetti and Stone and
Nick and Joe and Tony and Fritz . . . Some time I'm
going to write a book about New York, but this isn't it.
In a little more than two weeks, maybe a little more than
three, I was back in California, having done no Christmas
shopping. My agent met me at the airport, which meant
that he was proud of the deal he had made for me: a three
months' hitch at a thousand dollars a week. On the way
in from the airport the thing that kept depressing me was
that for three or four or five days I would not be able to
see a New York paper that I had not already read in New
York.

There were some ugly bills waiting for me at the hotel.
There were some swatches from some tailors, reminding
one that Palm Springs was in full swing and that the same
tailors who had the pleasure of serving Mr. William
Powell, Mr. Joel McCrea, Mr. Robert Taylor, and their
agents, would be pleased to meet one's Palm Springs re-
quirements. They would whip up a pair of whipcord
jodhpurs for a hundred dollars, and they begged leave to
call attention to the midnight blue evening tails, now the
accepted thing. Some excellent vintage wines had been
included in the latest shipment to arrive at Vendome
Spirits. Something new in supper club entertainment was
being offered at the Club Something on Sunset Boulevard.
Something new in night club entertainment was being
offered at another club on Melrose Avenue. On the other
hand, one's perennial favorites wanted to take the liberty
of reminding one that it was not too early to make one's
New Year's reservations at the Chez Something. Signed:
the perennial favorites. There were about a dozen un-
telegraphed telegrams, written by persons of originality
and taste (de gustibus non disputandum), inviting one to
cocktail parties at private houses, new artists' agencies,
and an automobile salesroom. There was an embossed,
stiff paper opportunity to have a party of four or six at a
dinner in honor of some Catholic big shot (my name got

me on a lot of Catholic sucker lists). All I had to do was
get up twenty dollars a plate. Black Tie. There were about
two dozen splendid opportunities to help The Cause, from
Tehachape to Tallahassee. There was a letter from my
mother, a reminder that my school endowment pledge
was unpaid, a request to straighten out an illegibly signed
check. There was a Dutch Kalendar from a swell girl in
Surrey, who wanted to be in plenty of time for Boxing
Day. There were a few telephone messages to be ignored.
And there was a note from Peggy.

It read:

James: It was nice of you to write me from New York,
you . . . A card or a telegram would have done (Heaven
knows you send enough of them for no good reason). But
this is not the kind of note I started out to write. Whenever you get back (some time this week, according to the
Hollywood Reporter) please phone me, unless you arrive
at an unearthly hour in the morning. As you may imagine,
this is serious. Love,

                                                    Peggy

P.S.: It is nothing to worry about from your point of
view.

                                                        P.

I read the note in my room. It was around lunch time,
so I phoned Peggy at the shop. For the first time in our
life I failed to recognize her voice. "May I speak to Miss
Henderson?"

"This is she. Is this you, Jim?"

Yes, sorry not to have recognized, etc. "I just got in.
Do you want to have lunch?"

"I always *do*. What kind of a New York expression is
that: 'Do you want to have lunch'? Of course I want to
have lunch."

"My but you're snippy. I think I'll go right out and
paddle that little round—"

"Yes, Mr. Bronson. I'll be glad to order it for you."

"I think I'll go right out and paddle those little round cheeks of yours, Miss Bronson. Would you like me to come out and paddle those little round cheeks of yours? Please be a little more respectful—"

"Thank you. I'll call you back," she said, and hung up. In a few minutes she phoned me. "Listen, you fool, the boss came in the shop and he could listen in on the extension."

"I'm sorry, I didn't know you had an extension."

"Is that another dirty remark?" she said.

"My God! What a really filthy mind! And you talk about me. You ought to be reviewing pictures for the Legion of Decency. Do you want to have lunch, *with me?*"

"If I can keep from throwing up. You make me sick. I'll meet you at the Derby, the Beverly one. Twelve-thirty."

It was only a short walk from her shop to the Derby. The boy parked my car in the lot across the street, and Peggy arrived by the time I got a table. That Derby is always so full of jabbering Beverly wives, pathetically dolled up as though for the Colony or Voisin, that it is a good place to talk privately, so long as you don't get caught in a lull. But some very funny things come out of those lulls. One time a woman was telling her companions a story, with her voice at the regular volume, and she got caught in a lull just as she was saying, ". . . I took opium." That was too bad, because she will spend the rest of her days telling people she never took opium.

Peggy was so pretty and sweet. She came in, took a quick look around and spotted me. It is easy to spot a man at lunch at that Derby. John, the headwaiter, brought her to the table.

"New coat?" I said.

"Twenty-five dollars, on the Boulevard. Plus tax. Do you like it?"

"It's the best-looking coat I ever saw. Twenty-five dollars."

"Yes. That makes it easy for me to tell you what I have to tell you."

"What have you done? Married Herbert? Let's see your ring."

"No. Nothing like that," she said. "After I wrote that note I tried to remember exactly what I said. It was a foolish note. Ill-considered. Inchoate."

"Whee!"

"I was a little worried about the effect it might have on you. I couldn't remember whether it had a postscript or not. I intended to write one but I wasn't sure I had."

"You did."

"Did you—were you afraid I was pregnant when you read the note?"

"Not after I read the postscript. What do you want to eat or drink, or be merry?"

"I think I'll have a straight whiskey. Rye. And a chicken salad, Russian dressing. Coffee with the salad. Melba toast."

"Did you get that, Bobbie?" I asked the waitress.

"Yes, Mr. Malloy. And you'll have?"

"A *sour* whiskey sour, not one of those banana splits. Corn beef hash without the egg, or *with* the egg. You know. Glass of some light beer."

"Thank you," said Bobbie.

"Okay. Well, what about the coat? Who gave you the coat, or how did you get it, or what's your story? So you won't talk, eh?"

"I'll talk," she said, with a nice smile. She lit a cigarette, scorning my assistance, because she liked to fool with those pull-out matches. She seldom smoked. "I got the coat from my father."

"Oh. Another check? Where from? Where's he spending Christmas?"

"Right where he is now. Right here. Seventy-two-sixty-eight Orchard Terrace."

"No!" I said. "Your father's here?"

"He's here, all right. In the flesh. Not a moving picture. Not a pretty picture, either."

"Peggy, what *is* this? Start from the beginning." Some-

how I always had thought of her father as about as real as
a character in some of the more entertaining virility fic-
tion in *The Saturday Evening Post*. Now and then there
would be an Anton Otto Fischer illustration of a story
that would make me think: that probably looks like Peggy's old man. Now my jealous first thought was: How
does she know it's her father? It's so long since she's seen
him. I was ashamed of that, but there it was.

"A week ago yesterday," she said, "Herbert brought me
home from the shop. He has a new car, and not that this
has anything to do with the story, but if T.B. doesn't get
him first, his driving will. I'm frightened to death to drive
with him, but he comes for me nearly every afternoon
and it's impossible to tell him how frightened I am. Most
likely you think he's insensitive and he is, to other people's feelings, but—I'm sorry.

"Herbert came up to the porch with me, and Millie
heard us and she came out looking frightened and began
whispering, 'Miss Peggy, there's a man here says he's your
father. He's been here most of the afternoon,' she said,
'and,' she said, 'I couldn't phone you because I was afraid.
He sat right beside the phone and I couldn't phone.' And
she said she wouldn't give him my address, meaning the
shop, and didn't know when I'd be back and so that was
that. So I went in and this man stood up and took a long
look at me and said, 'Peggy, I'm your father.' I knew he
was, too, right away. He knew me, too. It's true, Jim.
There were some vibrations, is the only way I can explain
it.

"Well, it was very embarrassing. Herbert, for instance.
He wouldn't have been much help, but he insisted on
coming in with me in case there was some trouble, so I
had to introduce him to this strange man. 'This is Herbert
Stern, Father,' I said."

"I never can remember Herbert's name," I said. "I'm
not even sure I ever knew it before."

"It was terribly embarrassing, but Herbert had sense
enough to leave, and my father and I sat there for an hour
or so. We had plenty to talk about, naturally, but we'd

finish one topic and we'd both sit there trying to think of what would be the next topic. Really, Jim. Have you ever had your father that you haven't seen for I forget how many years, suddenly return?"

"No, and I hope he doesn't. At least not on a dark night. Mine's been dead ten years or more."

"So was mine, really. Just think of it. It's an idea for a shocking short story. What if I were on a train, and this man decided I was nice-looking and I thought he was, and I let him pick me up and—so on. And he *is* at*tract*ive." She never used the word casually, but always as though she had carefully chosen it. "Or at least was this day. He was, well, if you can imagine Keith as he will be in about fifteen or twenty years or longer than that, but looking much younger than his age."

"What's he been doing all this time?"

"I'll come to that. We didn't really get into that the first few days he was back. That night Keith didn't come home until late and of course it would be the one night when he didn't call up and say he wasn't coming home to dinner. As a rule he's very considerate about those things. Then when he finally did come home. Oh, first my father wanted to take me out to dinner, to the best place in California, but I told Millie, she's darling, that we'd have dinner, my father and I, and to save something for Keith. Then after we had our dinner he wanted to know all about me and Keith. Then came the problem of where my father was going to sleep. That was embarrassing, but finally I had sense enough to ask him if he had his bags here or where, and he was stopping at the Hollywood Plaza, I think, and I insisted on his going to the hotel and getting his bags, but he refused and then he made a concession. He said he knew we probably weren't prepared for another person in the house that night, but he'd move over with us the next day, provided we had room. We have an extra room, so that was all right, although I'm glad he didn't stay the first night.

"Then he said he guessed I went to bed early on weekday nights, and he was saying goodnight when Keith arrived home. That was the worst part of that first day, because I could see Keith didn't take to him, immediately. He was surprised, and looked at my father as though he'd come from some other planet, and in very short time I could see Keith didn't like him. Of course Keith didn't show it, but I knew. I was glad to get my father out of the house.

"After he'd gone Keith didn't go to bed. I could see he expected to have a discussion about my father. You know Keith can suddenly get older and very mature. He started to smoke his pipe and look at me, waiting for me to start, but when I didn't he said: 'Well, what about him?' And I said *what* about him, and he said: 'What are we going to do about him?' And I said I couldn't think of what we were going to do about him, and then Keith wanted to know, just as though it were taken for granted, he wanted to know how we were going to get rid of him. Did we have to be polite? I said of course we'd be polite, but maybe my father's coming this way would change things entirely. Well, saying that was stirring up a hornet's nest. Keith was furious, as mad as I've ever seen him. 'Change things! It certainly will change things. He isn't going to stay in this house. He's never been our father, except the biological fact. He's never had any responsibility about us.' Meaning he'd never taken any. Keith said: 'We're not going to have him settle down here now, just because of some whim of his, or because he's afraid he's getting old and now he wants a home. You and I have a nice home of our own, and to hell with him. If he's planning to make our home his home, then I'm getting out.' Well, I never expected anything like this from Keith. In the first place I never realized that he thought anything about our home. It *has* been nice, but I never realized he appreciated it. I don't mean about gratitude, but in so far as being aware of what a nice home it was. I was touched, because we're a very undemonstrative brother and sister. I'm touched now, when I think of it."

I pressed her hand. She went on.

"'Well,' I said, 'maybe we won't have any difficulty

with him. Maybe he'll just stay a few days and he won't *be* any problem to us. Just control your feelings till we see what his plans are.' Then he wanted to know how I felt about my father. I keep calling him my father. Notice?"

"Yes," I said. "What do you call him when you're with him?"

"I try to avoid calling him anything, but I've been calling him Father. Anyway, when Keith asked me how I felt about my father I had to admit I didn't know, principally because I hadn't had time to form any conclusions, but when I began to think it over, to give Keith some kind of answer, I realized I didn't feel one way or another about him. Then. I do now." She stopped.

"And?" I said.

"I can't stand him. I wish he'd go away. If he doesn't go away soon and if your offer is still good, I'll marry you. Or I'll live with you without getting married. I've just got to get away."

"The offer's still good. If you want to be tentative, come and live with me until he goes away. Or, if you want money. Why not take some of that larcenous dough of mine? I have a new contract, three months at a grand a week. At Metro."

"I always said I wouldn't take any money from you, but this time I might. Thank you anyway, even if I don't, but I knew I could count on you, without your telling me. Not that that's what I wanted to see you about. Mainly I wanted to talk to somebody. I've talked a little to Karen, but she has her own troubles. Father lost his best advertising contract. Mother just out of the hospital. Kid sister raising hell in school."

"Well, here I am," I said. "Whatever I can do, and any time. I'm going to take a house in Beverly, and there'll be more than enough room. And if Keith wants to come with me, now or anytime, the house I'd like to have has a room in a sort of wing of its own, with a separate entrance and so forth. He could come and go as he pleased."

"I'll tell him," she said. "I guess I ought to get back to the shop, and I haven't even begun to tell you. Are you going to be busy about five-thirty? You could pick me up at the shop if you weren't. I want to tell you the rest of it, and I need some sex, too."

"Let's plan to have dinner. I'll get you a little tight and get you out of this. You're in bad shape, aren't you, my sweet?"

"Am I. Pay the check and walk with me to the shop."

6

IN SOME respects Philip Henderson was an older Don
Miller. Another way of putting it would be to say that
Philip Henderson was what Don Miller might easily turn
out to be if he continued his career. There are so many
men who live as Henderson had lived. Their stories can
never completely be told, for the reasons that it would
take a detective with an unlimited expense account to fol-
low them through the years, and since nobody cares that
much, no detective is likely to get such an assignment. It
would take a resourceful agent to check back on the story
as Henderson's kind would tell it. There are so many lies
in his version. Lies that he comes to believe himself.
There are gaps in time, too, that frequently can be explained by jail sentences. Henderson himself undoubtedly
had a criminal dossier or two, because there were two gaps
of a year or more in his story.

But this much we did come to know about him: he was
born in the '90's, in Buffalo, New York. His father was a
railroader, a divisional superintendent of maintenance
of way, which is a good railroading job. The Hendersons
were old New York State, dating back to pre-Revolution-
ary times. Henderson took pride in mentioning the fact to
Peggy and Keith, and was unable to understand their
apathy when this historical information was forthcoming,
as it frequently was. Philip, an only son, was sent to Cornell after high school. His college career was brief, and he
soon was fond of saying that he hoped Keith was getting
more out of college than *he* had. He was fond of saying,

47

too, that he had carved his name in Cornell history—on a table-top in a beer-drinking establishment in Ithaca. He said he just got sick of college one day, and said the hell with it and quit. I had heard the same thing said in about the same vague way by boys who I knew had been kicked out of school for petty thefts. It was rather hard to believe that he had been quite as gay in college as he said he had been. No man earning the salary of a superintendent of maintenance of way could have afforded such a son. He probably was gay enough, but not in the financial league that his stories put him.

After he quit college he came out to California to "grow up with the country." Through Masonic and railroading friends of his father's he got a railroad job in Los Angeles, which he used only to get started. After he got the lay of the land and made a few thousand friends he went into the real estate business. Everybody in California was in the real estate business in those days. He did well enough to convince a girl named Margaret Keith that she was getting a good thing in him. Besides, she loved him. So they were married.

When the United States entered the war Mr. and Mrs. Philip Henderson had a large bungalow several miles east of Hollywood. They also had a snappy car, a second-hand Mercer phaeton. Their friends were Angelenos and a few young married people in the Pasadena-Santa Barbara group, and now and then some of the Navy. The Hendersons quickly went into great debt, which was not lessened by the death of Mrs. Henderson's mother. They had presumed that when the sad day came, they would be at least out of debt, but it turned out that there was not much more left than it cost to put the old lady's remains under the ground. It was a disillusioning experience to young Philip Henderson. The least a woman can do is to do something for her only grandchild (for at that time Peggy was an infant).

The Navy first attracted Henderson when he decided to do his bit for Uncle Sam. The uniform, the cleanliness, the travel, the social life that his Navy acquaintances led, all were selling-points. But he had better luck getting into an army officers' training camp and it was as a second lieutenant of infantry that he went to France. After being shunted around here and there, always with the unhappy prospect of being assigned to the A.E.F. in Siberia, he was sent to France with a draft division, and he returned to California without having been shot either by the Germans or by his own men. He knew, of course, that in his absence he had become the father of a son. Also he rightly guessed that a deliriously grateful people had done nothing about his debts. A "college man," a successful realtor, a first lieutenant, a husband and father, he nevertheless was unable to command, as he put it, the kind of job he considered commensurate with his qualifications. He did not starve; a job selling real estate on straight commission, $50-a-week drawing account, kept food in the house. But it was not the large bungalow that he had left in 1917. That, like the Mercer and a lot of other things, had gone. Indeed, it became a piece of property that in his new job he once was asked to handle, but for sentimental reasons he asked another salesman to take it over.

It must not be inferred, however, that Henderson was all sentiment. He was not mawkish. In his service days he had come to face facts, such as the biological one that a man has to have a woman every so often. With Henderson it was pretty often, especially among the volunteers, the Junior League types who were there to run errands and things like that for the officers. In every good-sized city there were lovely young things in Sam Browne belts and beautifully cut uniforms. It was entirely up to you how far they could be persuaded to make a lonely and handsome young officer comfortable in what might be his last days on earth. Then there were women in France, and on the way to demobilization there were women at home.

And Henderson found out that there had been changes in his own home. His wife had had her hands full with the children and with the family finances. The presence of the children prevented her taking a job. She could not have made out financially by hiring a nurse. A nurse who was good enough for the babies would have taken all the salary the young and inexperienced wife could have earned. And in 1918 when the day came when she broke her last five-dollar bill, she went through a kind of terror that she never forgot. The next day she went to one of her rich Pasadena friends and borrowed a thousand dollars from him. He said he was glad to let her have it, and he meant it. He was married, and he had two children of his own and a mother who single-handed kept him out of the army, and he told Margaret that he felt it was the least he could do, etc. A few months later she had to go to him again, and again he gave her money; more than she had asked. Then the first thing they knew they were having an affair. She was grateful to him, and he got from her a sense of being needed. Twice, then, she had had to transfer her love away from her husband; once for her children, and the second time for her benefactor.

The first time Henderson asked her if she had remained faithful to him she told him about the man in Pasadena, without naming him. Henderson took it calmly, and without a cross-examination—she didn't care—he confessed that his own body had not been inviolate. Her confession did make it easier for him to get around as much as he liked, and then one day he did not come home. He wrote her from Chicago, saying he imagined that she guessed that there was nothing to her marriage, and he was good and God damn bored with the life of a husband. He said he imagined she would get along all right; the fellow in Pasadena now had a clear track. If she wanted to get a divorce, that was all right too. He had no great feeling about the children; he'd never known them, and to tell the truth he wasn't sure Keith was his child. . . .

The fellow in Pasadena was frightened when Margaret showed him the letter, but when she convinced him that there would be no fuss, that her husband did not know who he was, they resumed the affair; a pleasant relationship that continued for four years. It was convenient for him, and it was a financial life-saver for her. She was able to have a nurse for the children, which in turn enabled

her to go to business college and take a job in a department store. She became secretary to the head buyer of
ladies-ready-to-wear, and then she worked into selling in
the Paris Shop, a department that sold more expensive
clothes. Margaret Henderson was prematurely gray, just
a little on the stout side, and she was pretty in a way that
women liked. That is, she looked as though she belonged
where she was, a perfect saleswoman whom you would
almost but not quite invite on a trip to Del Monte or the
desert. She never bothered to divorce Henderson.

Henderson went only as far as Chicago with the woman
who took him away from Los Angeles. She was on her
way to New York a few days ahead of her husband. Together she and her husband were going abroad, and it
was fun for her and Henderson to have the week on the
train and in Chicago. She *was* a bit surprised when he said
he wasn't going back to Los Angeles, and she suspected
him of a form of blackmail when he borrowed some
money from her, but she had had a good time, and it was
an even chance that this would pay Henderson off. It did.

Now comes one of the gaps. Henderson's story as I have
put it down was pieced together from conversations we
had, he and I, and from things he told Peggy and Keith
and that Peggy knew from her mother. It may have been
presumptuous of me, but when Henderson turned up in
California I made a point of seeing a lot of Peggy. I was
nearer her father's age and his kind of life than anyone
Peggy knew, and I didn't want anything to happen to her,
so I saw a lot of Henderson. But of that, more to come.

This first gap, which Henderson not only left entirely
unexplained, but even ignored as though for two years he
had lived on air, may be traced to the Cook County
(Henderson called it Crook County) criminal records. I
don't know. Maybe he was skipping the gutter at that
time and had jobs that were so lowly that he had suc-
ceeded in forgetting them. Maybe he had been mixed up
in one of the many mobs that ran various localities in
Chicago. He never admitted that, but he did have a pretty
good account of the death of one of the greatest trumpet

players in jazz, a youngster who offended a mob guy and for punishment a couple of hoodlums rammed the neck of a beer bottle up his rectum. The pain drove this trumpet player crazy, his hair turned gray, and Henderson's story was that this fellow became a hophead, dying of an over-dose. Henderson told it almost as though he had been there all the time, and better than I'd ever heard it before.

He must have known some of the influential gangsters, because he once picked up the silverware in a Sunset Boulevard night club and told us to an odd penny how much it was worth. When we asked him how he knew, he said he had had a job selling silverware to restaurants, and he said something to me about I knew what kind of restaurants. He wouldn't come out and say speakeasy; he liked unnecessary intrigue as much as he liked the necessary kind that must have been a large part of his life.

I had been wrong about the gun-running in New Orleans. He explained that part of his odyssey: he had been associated with Huey Long. He said, "Huey had work for a man that didn't have a Southern accent." I imagined Huey had plenty of work for a man who didn't have a Southern accent, although it might have been awkward to use him, say, as a repeater at the polls. Henderson must have been there more than a few weeks, because he pronounced Pontchartrain and Louisiana and New Orleans the way they pronounce them down there. He also was a bore about oysters Rockefeller, and he knew somebody named Legendre. He admired Huey. He said Huey knew as well as anyone else that the every-man-a-king stuff was so much sheep-dip, but Henderson said he sincerely believed that if Huey had reached the White House he would have done a good job. He admired Huey in the same way a faithful employee admires a paymaster who has been shot in a futile attempt to protect the cash.

This story was given to us in short takes, as they say in the newspaper business. One part he always left out was the woman's angle. He would start a reminiscence about a wild party in Boston or Memphis or Dallas, and even when Peggy was not present he would tell it up to a certain point and we who were listening would have to supply the women. It never entered my head that there weren't always women in Henderson's life. I never failed to get (and never tried hard to avoid) the impression that Henderson always had a solvent woman to turn to when he was not in the money. Somehow you would picture Henderson arriving at Atlanta or St. Paul on a train that got in around ten p.m. He would take a taxi to the second-best hotel, walk up very pleased with himself to the clerk, register for a double room, and before unpacking he would be on the phone, fixing up a party for that night with a handsome brunette of thirty-six, whose alimony came regularly on the first or second of the month.

He had covered the country pretty thoroughly from Denver east, and twice he had done it legitimately; once as a sort of promotion and publicity man for a tire company that was sending a small fleet of gaudily painted cars on an advertising junket. Another time he was with the William Bradwell Smith Associates, which I knew of old. The William Bradwell Smith Associates put on drives, big and little. The biggest ones would be for the Community Chest of some of the largest cities. The smallest ones they handled were for hospitals and churches. The minimum "quota" for the minimum drive was $500,000, and the William Bradwell Smith Associates, practical philanthropists, would take care of the whole drive for a guaranteed 5% of the minimum, plus a bonus over the minimum for as much as the traffic would bear. The William Bradford Smith Associates, up to 1929, could turn any town in the United States into a frenzy of giving. The mayor, the "civic leaders," the clergy (sometimes excepting the Catholics), the press, the luncheon clubs—all would get into a lather. There would be a forty-foot "thermometer" in the Public Square; stickers on cars; consommé-veal-ice cream luncheons at a dollar a throw (in the Y.M.C.A. cafeteria or in the local branch of a hotel chain); prizes for the team captains (usually boarded cowhide luggage donated by an unregenerate harness dealer who was tired of looking at it); a daily Page One story headed M'NULTY LEADS

CHEST DRIVE, and two days before the drive ended Captain
or General or Doctor Somebody would announce that he
would give an additional, an *additional* $5,000 if that
amount were subscribed before the final dinner. And it
would be subscribed, thereby putting Middletowne over
the top and saving it from disgrace in the eyes of the
William Bradwell Smith Associates. In the picture I had
of Henderson and the alimonyed brunette the William
Bradwell Smith Associates played an important part. As a
William Bradwell Smith Associate, Henderson would
have met many of those handsome small-city women who
campaign because they have nothing else to do. And of
course when the Associates were running a drive for some
college he must have made contact with many a co-ed
alumna.

I could see Henderson in this, one of the more legitimate of his admitted enterprises during the '20's and '30's.
He would have learned the ropes under a veteran Associate, then he would be put on his own. I could see him,
even as I sat with him in Hollywood, getting up at one of
those luncheons. He was not a short man, but he was not
so towering tall that he would annoy the inevitable big
shot who was bantam in size. Henderson, like as not,
would stand up at the speakers' table. He would pick up a
spoon and beat a tattoo on two glasses of water—a tinkling
sound that was much more friendly than the rap of a
gavel. Ling-cling-a-ling-cling. Shuffling of chairs as team
members and captains faced the speakers' table. A sharp
short whistle as one eater signaled a waiter to get some
more coffee. The crack of silver-plate on heavy china as
another eater snapped his spoon through a block of Nea-
politan ice cream. Quantities of phlegm being pulled
from its resting place in a hundred throats. Then—attention. All eyes, except those of the man bolting his ice
cream, on Henderson.

Blue serge suit, two-button, ready-made, the coat open
to give an occasional hint of Henderson's Sigma Nu pin
under the upper left vest pocket. Soft white shirt with the
collar kept in place by invisible tabs. Two-dollar small-

figured tie. In front of him, on the table, a small pile of papers, which he arranged neatly until silence came. Then the surprise technique, which he would have figured out for himself. Instead of going immediately into his little talk he would call to the waiters in the back of the room. "Would you mind closing that door, please?" A volunteer would get up from a table and nod to a waiter and repeat Henderson's request, and then the volunteer would sit down, feeling as though he had rescued a family of five and their dog from a dangerous surf. He would be rewarded with a beautiful smile by Henderson, and a quiet but audible "Thank you." Then Henderson would cock his head and look at a far corner of the ceiling, causing the less alert ones to wonder what he thought he heard. The wise ones were sure he was considering how best to phrase today's good news. The man with the ice cream would put down his spoon and light a cigar.

Then suddenly: "This morning at the corner of Smithfield and Wood . . ." And Henderson was off.

7

IN THE few weeks between the return of Philip Henderson and the annual observance of the Birth of Christ, there were certain developments and adjustments chez Henderson. Among them:

More money in the Henderson household. Apparently Henderson had not come to Los Angeles broke. He first took Peggy on a shopping trip. He was paying cash, and she thought she might as well take what he offered. Outstanding household bills were paid, and Millie, the colored maid-of-all-work, was given a $3 raise to $18 a week.

Less seen of Keith at home. He moved to his fraternity house so that he could study later and still get enough sleep. That was his story. The truth was that he had not changed his opinion of his father. He urged Peggy to get everything out of Henderson that she could. The night Henderson said he had worked for Huey Long, Keith said: "Did you ever work for Zioncheck?" But Henderson refused to be insulted.

More seen of Herbert. Herbert had much the same protective impulse as mine. He was always around, it seemed. When Henderson would mention some "dirty Jew" in a story, and quickly apologize to Herbert, Herbert would say: "That's all right. I don't like all of them myself. You aren't compelled to like people just because of your being of the same blood." Henderson didn't get that.

No word of any kind from Don Miller. No word of any kind from Don Miller.

A lot of drinking. The first party was the Saturday night after Henderson began his visit. "Tonight's my night to howl," he announced at noon. Peggy usually worked Saturday afternoons, but her boss had given her the afternoon off to make up for the evenings she would have to work when the Christmas rush began, Beverly Hills being a good book customer at Christmas. I brought Peggy home after lunch that Saturday and Henderson made his announcement. Henderson gave Peggy fifty dollars. "Go out and buy yourself a slam-bang evening gown, and if that isn't enough, there's plenty more where that came from." Peggy said it was more than enough. "Well, just in case, here's ten more for a manicure and hairdresser. We're going places tonight. Oh, by the way, do you think you could scare up a girl for me?" Peggy was obviously shocked, and he said: "Doesn't have to be somebody my age. Get one of *your* friends." Later she said she was *afraid* that that was what he meant. She called her best friend, Karen Waner, who broke a date to come with us.

Henderson looked well in what he called a "Tuck." He had chubby cheeks, but no double chin, and his hair dried quickly and became very light brown, making him look not much older than I. His eyes were green. His teeth tight and even and all present from bicuspid to bicuspid. The missing teeth went unnoticed except when he laughed his heartiest.

When I arrived at the little house Henderson was shaking cocktails in a Coco-Malt shaker. It was a strange sight. In the many times I had gone to that house I never had seen three persons in evening dress all at once. Once in a great while Peggy and I would put on evening clothes, but on those nights there would be Peggy in an evening gown, waiting for me, and *only* Peggy and I. Now there were three: Peggy, her father, and Karen Waner. My coming made it four, and there were still more to come. Keith had found it simply impossible to go along. I forgot what excuse he offered; something unflattering and final, that had to do with college life. And so at the last minute Peggy had asked Herbert to come and bring a girl.

The Martinis were watery and had too much vermouth. No one noticed it. Henderson had the floor, and did not sit down at any time. He kept busy pouring cocktails and urging us to drink up. Karen had made a very good impression on him, which was not strange. Karen's father, a photographer, had a favorite subject, and it was Karen. If I had been a photographer she would have been mine, too. She was about two inches taller than Peggy and this night she had on a blue and white dress; blue, with large white flowers printed on it in just about the coloring of Wedgwood. In a way it was a bad dress, so far as the colors went. It was a pattern that did not show off her figure. But to make up for this lack it was cut low enough in front to offer at least circumstantial evidence proving that she had nothing on underneath. Her breasts were large, and then you noticed that her thighs were large, but she had good calves and ankles. She had one of the most exciting bodies I've ever seen, but even without that she would have been a knockout. She had a small head, heavily lidded brown eyes, small curling lips, and a short straight nose. She did not look older than Peggy. They didn't look as though their ages could be compared by the same standards. Peggy was definitely a young girl, about twenty years old. Karen was a young woman who happened to be the same age. She also made Henderson seem young, or at least inept.

Henderson was trying not to be too attentive to Karen, and wondering how much she knew about him and his return. But he was in a spot; Karen knew everything about him that Peggy could tell her, and always had. Karen loved Peggy, needed her, depended on her.

But Peggy was in a spot, too. Now that the party was a reality, she wanted it to go off well. She was pulling for everyone, and for the first time I saw her as a conventionally timid hostess. It certainly was a new side—Peggy, who could get up before a hundred persons and say what she was thinking about Tom Mooney or Harry Bridges, was being a conventional hostess.

"You a Californian, Miss Waner?" said Henderson.

"I was born here, but my mother and father are from back East."

"Whereabouts in the East?"

"Columbus, Ohio."

"Oh, yes. I've been there," he said. "Yes, Columbus. I have some good friends there. But I guess you wouldn't know them. Have you been there?"

"No, I never have."

"It's quite a place. Yes, I've been there several times. You ever been there, Mr. Malloy?"

"Just for a short time. I've driven through a couple of times. Stayed there overnight I think once."

"At the Deshler?" he said.

"Some name like that," I said.

"You know, you have some cousins living there, Peggy," said Henderson. "Your second cousins. I haven't seen them—well, before I came to California. I never looked them up." This, he realized, was a slight mistake. "Where you from, Malloy?"

"Gibbsville, Pennsylvania."

"Gibbsville. No, I don't think I've ever been there. Pittsburgh. Philadelphia, of course. Just where is that in Pennsylvania? Is it near Pittsburgh?"

"No. Nearer Philadelphia. In the hard coal regions."

"Oh, the *hard* coal regions. Miss Waner? Dividend?"

"Yes, please," said Karen.

"Say, I wonder if you're related to the ballplayers named Waner?"

"I don't imagine so. I never heard of them."

"You didn't? Play for Pittsburgh? I guess you're not a fan, then. In 1927, in the World Series. Peggy, how about you? Mr. Malloy?"

Herbert arrived along about this time. In tails, and with a very tall Jewish girl, taller than he. Instinctively I knew that Miss Harris—Joan was her first name—was going to be my problem. She had good conventional manners and probably was a distant cousin of Herbert's. She accepted a cocktail without a word and took a quick look around, which was all she needed, and then settled down.

She gave her attention to anyone who was speaking, and in between she would stare at Karen. I was thinking up a plan to snub her when Karen stared back at her, and then Joan smiled and it was a nice smile. After that I liked her. But she didn't help much in conversation.

"Well," said Herbert, after he told Henderson he didn't drink, "how do you like California? Oh, I forgot you've been here before."

Henderson gave three chuckles. "Well, this *is* all pretty new to me. By George, they certainly have done some building in the last eighteen, twenty years. You live here, Miss Harris?"

"Just for the winter. My home is in New York."

"Oh, is that so?"

"Mr. Henderson, Joan and I have a friend," said Herbert. "He'd like to join us later. Would you mind telling me where we'll be around half past eleven, twelve?"

"Why didn't you bring him along? Call him up and tell him to join us now. Extra man. I hardly ever dance, the girls—"

"Thank you, but he has an engagement for the early part of the evening. Joan's going up to San Francisco tomorrow and he wanted to see her."

"Well, I don't know. Peggy, where do you think we'll be around that time?"

"Ho-ho. Don't ask *me*," said Peggy.

"Why, of course I'll ask you, Peggy. What's the best place, after dinner? The Trocadero's about the only place I know of."

"Well, in that case you better ask Jim to get us a table, Saturday night."

"Will you do that, Mr. Malloy?"

"Sure. Be glad to, but I don't think we'll have to. The headwaiter's a friend of mine."

"Well, whatever you say. Mr. Stern, you tell your friend it would be a pleasure if he'd join us at the Trocadero."

"Tell him to ask for my table, Herbert," I said.

"All right, but remember, Mr. Malloy, this is my party. I want that understood before we start. Huh?"

"Sure," I said.

"Don't you think we'd better get started, Father?" said Peggy. "Jim, we can all go in your car, can't we?"

"Sure," I said.

"I'll take Joan in mine," said Herbert. "Both of us have to be home early."

And so we went to Lamaze and had a good dinner and everybody got tight, everybody but Herbert. Some ate filet mignon and some ate squab. All had champagne. Everybody danced, including Herbert, who was grim and silent with Joan, and loquacious with Peggy. He didn't dance with Karen. Henderson danced with each girl in turn. It was quite a workout for me, and only less so for Henderson. An armful of Karen made me forget that platonic basis we were on, and after I danced with Joan I told myself that if I weren't being temporarily faithful to Peggy I would certainly investigate Miss Harris. She liked to dance that way. When people bumped us out of that position she would settle back into it. Watching her face whenever she danced with Henderson, I was reminded of an engineer and a locomotive; his head sticking out of the cab was Intelligence; but it was the locomotive that was doing the work.

You could say to Karen: "Well, what about it, Karen?"

And she would say: "Why ask, when you know the answer?"

"Well, you might change your mind."

"I know. Let's go to bed together and see what happens. *That* old stuff."

"I warn you. You're taking the wrong attitude. I'll never make you a big movie star when I get to be a producer."

"You'll never make me, period," she said. "Besides, I'm no good. They all tell me that. A man like you, with all your experience, you'd want somebody to be very good. So. By the way, I hear you're out of the unemployed class."

We often talked that way, and the thing was, that kind of talk was full of truth. I liked Karen, and the things I

said I meant, but without any optimism. Peggy knew all
about Karen, and what I knew about her Peggy had told
me. Their good friendship had begun when they were
together in high school. It had the little beginnings: Peggy
thought Karen was the prettiest girl in school, and with
her usual generosity, said so. Karen was a pretty but
frightened freshman of a few days, and when she heard
what Peggy said she remembered that she *was* pretty.
With this renewal of confidence in herself she was able to
go out of her way to make friends with Peggy, and in a
month or so each knew what the other was doing every
hour of the day. So it had continued. Peggy, in her way,
needed Karen. Peggy was not a pretty freshman; whenever she wanted to she led her class, but she was a rather
fat little thing. She had no beau. Then the boys began to
see that if they were going to get to Karen, it had to be
through Peggy, which was how Peggy became a non-virgin.
It was hardly more than a technical knockout for the boy
who accomplished Peggy's change of status. There were
no ill effects; in fact, only a great curiosity and surprise
that there were no effects at all. Peggy often said she
waited for someone to notice the change in her, but no
one ever did. Even the first boy didn't realize or believe
that he was the first. She promptly told Karen, who more
or less promptly determined to change her own status;
but in Karen's case there were effects. The first time was
bad, and there was a frightened, hated boy, and a frightened, miserable girl. Then for Peggy a good adolescent
love with a good, slightly older boy, but for Karen the
next time—a year or so later—was as bad as the first; she
had to have an abortion.

They lived near each other, and after high school the
friendship was even better than it had been. They didn't
have to see each other every day, as was the case in school,
but hardly ever did two consecutive days pass without
their being together.

Henderson paid the bill and we moved down Sunset
Boulevard to the Trocadero. John, the headwaiter, whom

I had known in New York night clubs, gave us a table in the second row from ringside. More champagne, and more dancing. Henderson was duly impressed with the movie stars, and completely unimpressed with the directors, not one of whose names he recognized, so I gave up trying to point out local celebrities who were not actors. Fan magazine photographers, trade paper owners, agents, brothers and sisters of the stars, visiting musicians, producers, press agents, Los Angeles politicians, and a large and rather badly behaved group of Pasadena-Santa Barbara younger set meant nothing to him, and they were the people I spoke to. I didn't know any star there well enough to introduce Henderson. I said: "Sometimes the stars sit downstairs in the bar, if you'd like to meet some. I might know someone downstairs. I'll take a look."

"Oh, that's all right," he said "I've met some of them. Not the present-day ones. Wally Reid. I used to know Wally. Norman Kerry. There was a well-built chap."

"Well, I'll take a look." I went downstairs to the bar, not to do Henderson any favor, but to take a look around for my agent, who I was fairly sure would be there. But on my way to the bar I saw good old Don Miller, sitting in a booth. I immediately recognized the girl with him, and so would have at least half the men in the room. She was one of the girls; a free-lance. Miller was paying his bill, and he saw me. "Malloy, old boy. How the hell are you?"

"All right," I said. "Hello, dear."

"Huh. I didn't think you'd remember me," said Dear.

"How could I forget you?" I said. She was all right, but sometimes a trouble-maker when she got drunk and remembered that she had been Miss Potter County Texas or something.

"Just paying my check," said Miller. "How about a quick one. You're all duked out. What's it, a party?"

"Mm-hmm. Upstairs." I sat down. "What's with you?"

"You mean Charlotte?"

"No, I don't mean Charlotte. I wouldn't refer to Charlotte that way, would I, dear?"

"I don't know how you'd refer to me and I'm sure it doesn't concern me in the least how you refer to me."

"Oh, it's that way," I said. "Okay."

"You shut up," said Miller to Charlotte. "This is my pal. My pal Malloy, huh, Malloy?"

"If you say so," I said. "Scotch and soda."

"St. James, Mr. Malloy?" said the waiter.

"Yes. Oh, hello, Franz. Well, kid, you must be doing all right."

"You mean Charlotte," he asked.

"No, I don't mean Charlotte. That's twice I don't mean Charlotte. I mean the Troc and so forth. Where you living?"

"Same place."

"Where are *you* living, dear?"

"I'm living in Honolulu, where do you think I'm living? Are you trying to pretend you don't know where I live? I suppose I'm not good enough for you in the Trocadero. Hunh. You don't have to take that attitude, *Mis*-ter Malloy."

"I don't think she likes me," I said. "I think I'll have my drink at the bar. Give me a buzz, kid. I'll be at Metro from now on."

"She's a little drunkie," said Miller. "I'll be seeing you."

I picked up my highball and went to the bar, and Miller and Charlotte departed. I talked to the bartender while I drank my drink, forgot about my agent, and rejoined the party upstairs.

In my absence they had decided to go some place else, but agreed to wait ten more minutes for Herbert's friend. In those ten minutes I had a strange conversation with Henderson. It began when I explained to Peggy that I had met Miller downstairs: "*Don* Miller. You met him." She remembered him.

"Don Miller? What Don Miller?" said Henderson, who I thought was busy with Karen's garter.

"You wouldn't know him," I said. "He's a kid—I beg your pardon. A young fellow from back East."

"Where from? Washington, D. C.?" said Henderson. "I

knew a Don Miller there. What business is this fellow in?"

I didn't know whether to make up a whole new story to protect Miller, or to give Henderson some truth, or to stall. I stalled. "I don't know just what business he *is* in."

"How old a fellow is he?"

"Oh, I don't know."

"About twenty-four," said Peggy. "Wouldn't you say?"

"Somewhere around there," I said.

"What kind of a looking fellow is he?" said Henderson.

"Handsome. Tall, dark, and handsome," said Peggy, giving a very bad imitation of Mae West.

"It couldn't be the fellow you know, Mr. Henderson," I said.

"I don't think so either," said Peggy. "This boy is from Jim's home town."

"Oh, from Pennsylvania," said Henderson.

"That's the name of the *state*," I said. "No, this couldn't be the same guy. Peggy, how about a jig?" We danced.

I was not satisfied that Henderson was satisfied. I realized that I must have seemed unnecessarily evasive. If Henderson knew the Donald Miller on whose traveler's checks my Don Miller, or Schumacher, was living, he might also know about the checks. It was too bad that I hadn't told Peggy the real story of Miller, but it seemed better now not to take a chance.

We waited about twenty minutes for Herbert's friend, and he did not show up, so Herbert took Joan home. She was in a bad temper on account of her dilatory friend. Karen and Peggy and Henderson and I went to a couple of other places, to see Jerry Bergen and Louis Prima, and then I took them to their homes.

When I got home I called Don Miller and after a long wait a sleepy voice said he didn't think Mr. Miller was home, because his key was in the box. I left a message, but I had no hope of its ever being delivered or even written down. Then I called Charlotte's number, but no answer. I reread parts of Zola's "Germinal," stopping every half hour or so to telephone Charlotte. About five-thirty she answered.

"Charlotte, this is Jim Malloy. Is Miller there?"

"Oh, it's you. What do you think this—"

"This is important. If Miller's with you, I have to speak to him."

"Go —— yourself," she said. "You can't high-hat—"

"Tell Miller it's about Washington," I said.

"What'd he do, cross the Delaware?" she said, and hung up.

I tried to get her back, but she left the phone off the cradle. Of course there were two or three things I might have done—but there were reasons why I couldn't send her a telegram or go to her house, because I didn't know her last name, and I didn't know her address. She often had come to my house, but I never had been to hers. All I knew was that it was a three- or four-dollar taxi ride from a house I'd had in Beverly Hills, which wasn't much help. The best I could do was to send Miller a telegram to his house, which I did.

8

THE NEXT day I awakened five or six times with an inexplicable hangover; inexplicable in that I had not been drunk the night before. No blank periods; I remembered everywhere I had been, everyone I had spoken to, everything I had done. It may have been that I drank too much without getting stewed. Whatever it was, I had a hangover, and I awakened five or six times, dozed off again, changed my position in bed in the hope of getting rid of the throbbing headache. It was no use.

It was the middle of the afternoon. I sent down for a big orange juice and scrambled eggs and coffee and oatmeal and the Sunday papers. The eggs were not done the way I like them, but I put away the rest of the food and presently, after the usual natural functions, I felt well enough to tackle Miller on the phone. He was home.

"Say, what was the idea of calling me at Charlotte's? I call that a pretty lousy—"

"Listen, you punk, I don't care what you call it. You listen to me. I think you're in a real jam. You better come on out here and I'll tell you about it."

I read Louella and her daughter and W. R.'s editorial, and studied my favorite study, Ginger Rogers in color, and second-guessed the eastern football scores, and got mad about the latest ex-Communist who was telling all, and won a bet with myself that my name would not be in a list at a party I'd gone to, and read the second-hand automobile classifieds (but no Alfa-Romeo for $450 cash), and saw a fairly good wisecrack I had made three years before attributed to a New York orchestra leader, and read the titles of the Sunday sermons, and tried to calculate how much I would make if I were a sports writer again and on the take. I thought, as I thought every day, of the Paramount writer who came home from the studio one day and saw his father reading the paper. "What's in the paper, Dad?" he said.

"Huh," snorted the old man. "L. A. dog chases L. A. cat over L. A. fence."

I thought of Ginger and wondered how many youths at Yale and Kenyon and Stanford and Texas Christian and St. Bonaventure's and Clemson and Magdalen and McGill and Bowlder and Yale-in-China were thinking of her at just that minute. And the next minute I was sending flowers to Peggy. I had the clerk say on the card: These are New York Cut. Then the phone rang and it was Miller. He came up.

"Sit down," I said. "Want some coffee? Get the glass out of the can."

He got the glass from the bathroom and I filled it with coffee. He drank some, put the glass on the desk and lit a cigarette. "What's the jam I'm in?" he said.

"I *think* you're in one," I said. "Let me think how to begin this.

"Well, suppose I begin this way. I'll give you the worst part first. The facts. Then you can help me figure out if you're in a jam. Last night when I saw you at the Troc, one of the guys upstairs on the party I was on, when I came upstairs I happened to mention I saw you. I was with the Henderson girl. You met her with me that night at the South Seas."

"Sure, I remember her. Nice little number."

"Sure. Well, I mentioned your name, and immediately this guy wanted to know *what* Don Miller. From Washington?"

"Jesus!" said Miller.

"So I started to say I didn't know where you were from, but Peggy, the Henderson girl, she said you were from Pennsylvania. Then this guy wanted to know what business you were in. I said I didn't know. I said I didn't know you very well."

"Who was the guy?"

"And I told him I didn't know how old you were, but she volunteered the information that you were around twenty-four or -five."

"Who was he?"

"Just let me tell you the story, will you? Then he wanted to know what you looked like, and we gave him a sort of stall, but maybe not enough of a one. Peggy said you were tall, dark, and handsome, like Cary Grant in that Mae West picture."

"Jesus." He put his face in his long fingers and sat like a kibitzer or a condemned man. "Well, who was this guy?"

"I don't know whether to tell you or not. I don't know whether it'll do any good to tell you."

"God damn it, sure it will, Malloy. Give me a break."

"I'm giving you a break. These L. A. cops are tough, you know. I could just as easily be held as accessory after the fact or something, just sitting here talking to you. In my room, don't forget. All right, I'll tell you who it was. It's Peggy Henderson's father. He suddenly blew into town the other day."

"Jesus!"

"They don't know much about him, she and her brother. He disappeared when the brother was a kid, about fifteen, twenty years ago, give or take a couple years. Since then he's been traveling around the country, practically every place but out here. Different jobs. Advertising. I sat in on one session with the guy, and he's told his kids a few things, but I don't think he's a cop. Still, he may be. Not a regular cop. Maybe some kind of a special dick. An investigator. One of those. Maybe he works for that American Express or American Bankers or whatever it is. The people that issued those checks of yours."

Miller took one hand from his face and made a fist and pounded the air. "Oh, God."

"What?" I said. "The heat's on?"

"I guess so."

"What are you going to do? What are your plans?"

"Screw out of here, that's the first thing," he said.

"It might be a very good idea, but where, and how? Have you any dough?"

"Uh-huh. A couple hundred bucks. I owe a little, not more than fifty bucks. I don't know where to go though. Get a job on a ship, maybe."

"How? You've never been to sea, you don't belong to any union, and I wouldn't advise you to do any scabbing out here. But how do you know this Henderson is after you? It might be just a false alarm, or maybe he does know this Don Miller, maybe he's an older guy. All you have to do is change your name again, quietly leave this part of the country and go back to Swedish Haven or wherever you please."

"No, I got a hunch on this. This is it, all right. See, Malloy, they have my description everywhere I cashed one of those checks, and another thing, my pal in Washington, they probly got a description from him, so they'll be looking for me at Swedish Haven. So I can't go there, and I can't be Schumacher again, either. And there's something else makes me think this is the right guy. I mean by that, makes me think he's a detective. God damn it!"

"What's that?"

"Well, you were pretty swell to me so I might as well let you in on it. I cashed another check."

"Oh, you damn fool. What'd you do that for?"

"That bim I was with last night. Charlotte."

"Why, you dope, you didn't have to—why, she's a—she isn't any two-buck whore, but you could have been on the free list."

"Better'n that. She wanted to keep me. But I picked her up one night and I gave her this line of crap. I told her my old man was a big-shot banker in New York and I was out here to learn the business end of the movies. So I started in spending dough on her. I *was* on the free list, that's true, but I would of done better just giving her ten or twenty bucks every time I laid her. I spent that much on her every time I went out with her."

"Why?"

"I do' know. I liked her. Maybe she is a whore, but. Well, you laid her. I had to have more dough, see? I put on this act, banker's son and all that. I bought a new Ford. Aah." At this point I thought he was going to cry. "I was only sore last night because I thought you were trying to get her to come out, or you come down to her place."

"Nope," I said. "Last night was the first time I saw her since, oh, last summer. Are you in love with her?"

"I don't know. I never exactly thought of it that way. That's something I never was, in love with any girl. But she's all right. She often says to me, 'We don't have to go out.' She says I probly get a small salary and hardly any allowance and I don't have to spend it on her. That's what she said after she saw the joint where I live."

"Can you tell her the truth? Is she in love with you?"

"She offered to give up hustling for me."

"Maybe she'd be glad of the chance if she thought you could keep her. What do you honestly think? Is she in love with you enough so that you could trust her?"

"Well, it's so hard to say. Sometimes I think she is, but then I don't know. The first night I was with her, I went crazy. I never had anything like it. I thought, this dame must be nuts for me. She tells me I'm the only guy she ever enjoyed it with. We'll be walking along the street together or in a movie, and all of a sudden she'll start in, only talking. The other night we went to the movies and we no sooner got inside than she started in, did I like it last night, did I want to do it that way with the dame in the picture. Till I couldn't see straight."

"I guess you must be all right in the hay," I said.

"No, it's her. And she's only from Texas, only a plain ordinary American. Pretty, but, you know."

"Sure. Well now, listen, anything to get off the subject of tail, or I'll be sending down for the operator or somebody. Here's what I suggest. You figure out whether you can trust this Charlotte or not. That's entirely up to you.

If you have any doubt about it, the hell with her. Don't
see her any more, because she can be trouble. I imagine
the cops know her, otherwise she wouldn't be able to
operate even if she didn't have a record. As far as I know
she's honest, and has no record. But they might be able to
trace you through her, if they're going to trace you. Now
what you do, you get rid of that car. Get out of that place
where you're living and move to some place way the hell
away from here, like on the other side of Western Avenue,
or else go to Long Beach or any place, but don't stay
around Hollywood or Beverly or any of these places.

"Change your name, and get a job. Get some kind of
job that isn't a white collar job. Car-washer. Take any
kind of dough, just to get a job. You have enough to stake
you for a while, and if you need dough later I'll lend you
some. Only don't get the idea that I'm going to keep you.
How're your eyes?"

"Good, I guess."

"Well, go to some cheap jewelry store where they ex-
amine eyes and they'll find something wrong with them.
They always do. Nobody has perfect eyes out here, and if
one of these oculists saw perfect eyes he'd think there was
something wrong with them. Get yourself a pair of glasses
with steel rims, not tortoise-shell. Tortoise-shell look
phony sometimes."

"Were you ever on the lam?"

"That's none of your business," I said. "I write for the
movies, and whether I was on the lam or not doesn't make
any difference. Another thing. You have to cultivate a
new personality. Dress differently. Get yourself a cheap
suit that doesn't fit so well, a coat that doesn't cover your
ass. Did you pay cash for your car?"

"Yes," he said. "Traded the old one and the rest cash."

"Sell it at a loss, to get rid of it quickly. Maybe you
ought to get a motorcycle, second-hand. That would certainly be a new thing in your personality. While I think
of it, don't ever call me here. It's safer to call me at the
Studio. Let me know where you are, but don't get in

touch with me except when it's absolutely necessary. Will you remember all this?"

"Yes."

"Don't forget it. I want to tell you something. You know, this may be a false alarm. But even if it is it'll be a good thing for you to change your identity again. If it'll make you feel any better, I *was* on the lam once, in New York, and I threw off the people that were after me by pretending to leave New York, but all I did was move to another hotel a block away, by way of Grand Central. Well, I guess that's all I have to offer."

"Well Malloy, I sure appreciate your kindness. I—"

"Skip it. By the way, where did you cash this last check?"

"At some gambling joint. They knew Charlotte and she told them my old man was a banker. All—"

"What gambling joint? The Surf?"

"Yes," he said. "It's *some place.*"

"My boy," I said, "you want to get the hell out of this section as fast as you can. You're in the middle, between the law and the mob guys. Beat it, and good luck."

He left, and I sat there in comfort, thinking about him and how I came to know him. The town he came from was a few miles from my home town, but it might as well have been a few states away, for all the mixing the people of the two towns did. As a reporter it was my job to know people like his father and all the other ministers, undertakers, cops, justices of the peace, politicians, station agents and other news sources. But this kid himself was not important enough to know, even though I had once written his name, wrong. Probably the only way he would ever get to be known outside of his home town was the way another townsman of his had become notorious. This other fellow was a sort of bush-league public enemy, who held up a dozen banks and filling stations before he was accidentally killed by a West Virginia deputy sheriff. The deputy didn't sound like the kind of minion of the law who goes around routing out public enemies. Anyway, this public enemy turned out to have been born in Swedish

Haven, although he hadn't lived there from the age of two on. It gave us a good one-day story, and it made Swedish Haven feel that the eyes of the world were upon it, the way such towns feel when the local Elks take the lead from all the cities of that size in new members gained during the month of October, and get written up in the *Elks Magazine*. Or when the high school relay team wins its event at the Penn Relays. Or when some obscure housewife wins a Plymouth sedan for the very best last line to a prepared advertising limerick, and her name and address are announced over the radio.

And yet to me this kid was a sort of celebrity, the way anyone is who is wanted by the law. Sitting there in my room he was a frightened kid, the same age as one of my brothers, and he was about as unexciting a figure as there was in Los Angeles County. But the moment he left the room he began to be different. Already I was *remembering* him, not seeing him, and what I remembered was a figure that had passed, like a celebrity who has been pointed out to you just as he passed, so that you don't see his face but only his back. Miller was a tall young man, whose rounded shoulders contributed to the picture of a hunted man. All hunted men have rounded shoulders, in your mental picture of them. Sometimes they are turning their heads over a shoulder. I hoped Miller would get out of his own jam without any help from me, but that he would I neither doubted or believed.

I put on a new brown double-breasted suit and a blue shirt and brown foulard tie and an old pair of brown Scotch grain brogues. I left the coat hanging until I had called Peggy and told her I would take her for a ride. She told me to come right over.

She was alone. She said her father had gone out to have a demonstration of a second-hand LaSalle that he was thinking of buying. He had wanted her to come along, but she said she expected a call from me, which was nice of her, as I had not mentioned that I would call.

"Oh, I just used you as an excuse is all," she said. "I

don't want you to think of me sitting all alone by the telephone."

"Waiting for a ring, a ting-a-ling. Well I'm glad you waited, and I'm glad I called."

"And I'm glad you sent me flowers. Why don't you do that oftener?"

"I don't know."

"New York Cut," she said. "Oh! I just got it! You meant the steaks. Of course, of course, how stupid of me."

"No," I said. "You're *used* to seeing it, and it's still new to me."

"Why don't you send them oftener? I *know* why, of course."

"Why?"

"Well," she said, "if you were in love with Karen I'll bet you'd send her flowers, all the time. Every day when Karen came home there'd be a little box of flowers with some witty note."

"Not a witty note every day. Flowers maybe, but—"

"Yes, you'd try anyway. But with me—I'm not a glamor girl like Karen. I'm not beautiful. I'm a mere, oh, I don't know. Slightly pretty. Slightly intelligent. Pushover for you."

"Now don't talk like that, Peggy."

She laughed her fat little laugh that began low and went high and came back to low. "All right. But I'm a woman. Remember that. And I like to receive flowers. I may not *like* flowers, but—"

"Oh. So you don't like flowers. That's what you're carping about." I pretended to ignore her, and the first thing I knew I was ignoring her. There was a car ahead of us—we were driving out Wilshire by this time, with Malibu vaguely in my mind—and it was a convertible sedan like mine, with a low top so that I couldn't see who was in it. But the radio was on rather loud and it was playing something that I liked. It might have been the Toccata and Fugue, or it might have been the Three Oranges march, or it might have been Stack o' Lee Blues. It was something I liked and did not expect to hear from a California car on a Sunday afternoon on Wilshire Boulevard. It was the kind of thing that I expected every Californian to turn off. I switched on my own radio and tried to find the station that the other car had.

"You hurt?" said Peggy.

"Shh!" I monkeyed with the radio. "Trying to get something."

"You'll get something. A sock on the head if you shush me."

"Peggy, I'm trying to get the station that those people have. The Chrysler. The car like mine."

"I thought this was a Buick."

"It is. Please." I couldn't find the station, and then I got a break in traffic and drew up alongside the Chrysler. In it were four people: two girls, two young men. "What station have you got?" I said.

"I beg your pardon?" said the girl who was driving.

"I wanted to get that tune. What station are you tuned in on?"

They told me. It was one of those stations that broadcast nothing but phonograph records. I tuned in and it was what I wanted. Then the light changed. I was enjoying myself, and after I changed gears I reached over and took Peggy's hand. She took it away. "Wasn't that rather obvious?"

"Can't I hold your hand?"

"You know what I mean. I've seen you practically sock somebody that just looked at me when I was with you, but you, you drive right up to a girl on Wilshire Boulevard. What nerve! If I'd been one of those men . . ."

"Oh, balls!" The anger came first. Later I would be pleased that she was jealous. Now it was so unreasonable and so petty feminine that I wanted to hit her. "You must be getting change of life or something. I wanted to hear that music, and I thought the kind of people that listened to that music wouldn't mind if I asked them. I thought—well, what the hell."

"Don't try to explain it. You simply saw a pretty girl

and so you picked a fight with me and *drove* the car fifty miles an hour through traffic to catch up with her, and then you couldn't think of anything better to say than, 'I beg your pardon, but as one music-lover to another I know I can't pick you up now, but if I see you again at the Trocadero will you remember me because you're very pretty and we have this mutual love of good music. Isn't it wonderful? Two souls, brought together by our passion for Bach!' "

"Who writes your dialogue? And what an actress! Boy, when you want to turn on the histrionics. I'll bet you wowed Hollywood High in Paolo and Francesca, or Green Stockings."

She burst out laughing, and she couldn't stop. "Well?" I kept saying. "What was it? Come on, what did I say?" I soon was laughing myself.

When she stopped laughing, she said: "I was *in* Green Stockings." Then she put both hands on my shoulder and it was all right after that. I kissed her and we were quiet. We turned off Wilshire and drove slowly up Rodeo Drive and across Carmelita and up Roxbury to Sunset and then back to Rodeo and down and around and around, and I said: "Pick a house. Look for one around three-fifty or five hundred. I'm going to rent a house, the hell with this hotel life."

"I wish you did have a house. I don't like where you live now. I don't like anything about it. I'd rather live where I live. You could have a house like ours and two servants for what you pay now, and still save money. Too many people can see me going in and out of your place. But I thought you had one picked out."

"I did, but I want you to pick one *you* like."

"If you live out here—well, the capitalists have got you at last. If they didn't always have you."

"Oh, yeah?" I said. "I lived here before, remember." Then I drove her around and pointed out houses that were owned or rented by the leftists in the movie colony. She pointed out houses that were owned by the reactionaries. "Sure, sure," I said. "I concede all that. My only point was that if the nice guys can live in these houses and still be nice guys, why can't I? Couldn't you?"

"I'd always be thinking of how much I could save by living somewhere else, and sending the difference to the Loyalists or the Scottsboro boys."

"You better learn to like this part of town, because you're going to live out here."

That afternoon we didn't do much more driving. I called up a movie writer I knew who had a house in Beverly, and he was going away and I borrowed his house. Late that night I told Peggy my suspicions of her father, and Miller's story, and she promised to find out what she could.

9

THE NEXT day I started my new job at Metro and the second day I was there I acted on an impulse, the overwhelming kind that I always got when I started a new job: the impulse to spend money in a big way. I left the studio that afternoon and drove over to a real estate agent I knew, picked out a house in Beverly for five hundred a month, had the agent hire a Negro couple, and the next day I moved in. I called for Peggy at the shop that day and behaved with all the mysteriousness I could summon. We drove in, stopped the car in the driveway, and I got out and said: "Come on, get out."

"What's this all about?"

"Get out."

She got out and I picked her up and carried her to the door and rang the bell, and Jonas, the Negro, opened the door and I carried her in, to the amusement of Jonas, who then left. I kissed her hard before putting her down. "I love you," I said. The strange thing was that that was impulse too; I had had no intention of saying it. I put my arms around her and kissed her again, long.

"Oh, Jim," she said. "This is the way to do it. Here, hold me here. Let me hold you. I want you. Where do we go?"

On the way upstairs we stopped again. She was two steps higher than I and I held her with my arms around her thighs. "It's like a first time, only better, isn't it?" she said.

"It is a first time, darling," I said. "Say it."

"I love you. I always loved you. I'm so excited. Let's

79

stand here and think of what we're going to do. Let's talk about it. Do you know what I'm going to do to you?" She whispered.

"Let's do it now," I said. I was getting superstitiously apprehensive. I was in a hurry to have the first time accomplished. She kissed my forehead and turned and began running up the remaining steps. She took things off as she ran; her jacket, her sweater. She turned around and looked at me only once. I never had been so excited in my life—and ten minutes before I had only intended to show her the house. There was something new in her eyes. She seemed younger, too, and with her hands she was discovering her own body while she watched me. "Is it true about Chinese women?" she said.

"No."

"How do you know?"

"Well, it isn't true about Japanese women. I do know that."

"Oh, you do, eh? What about colored women?"

"Don't know anything about them. What about you, is it true about you?"

"Stop talking and hurry up."

"Yes," I said. She was right; this was one time when we could do without the talking and joking that we always did. Later on, when she was finishing a cigarette, we did talk.

"How much does this place cost?"

"Five hundred."

"Goodness! How long'd you take it for?"

"Three months."

"Has it got a swimming pool?"

"No. What good would a swimming pool be this time of year? You must have been reading the ads, the Year Round Club ads."

"You'll have to get a double bed. I don't like twin beds."

"I think there is a double bed in one of the other bedrooms. In fact I know there is. But I like this room better than the one with the double bed."

"I guess most people don't need as much room as we do. Otherwise twin beds wouldn't be so popular. The furniture is nice. Whose house is it?"

"I have to think. It's a strange name. A long German name. They aren't picture people. The husband came out here for Ford or General Motors, and I think he's been transferred. The rest of the house is nice, too. There's a pool table."

"Is there a nursery? I may need one after this."

"Oh, Peggy, you must know by this time I'm sterile."

"You mustn't be. Don't you want children?"

"I do if you do. I have no great feeling about perpetuating the name. I have enough brothers to take care of that."

"I wonder how I'd be as a mother."

"Wonderful," I said. "I really mean that."

"Why? What makes you think so?"

"You're sweet and kind and intelligent, and passionate. I think you have to be to be a good mother. I don't know, your breasts are so good."

"I used to hate them. I had them when I was fourteen, almost the same size as they are now. They are nice, aren't they? What do you like best about a girl's figure?"

"Her breasts."

"Not here?"

"Sure, but breasts mostly. Are you psycho-analyzing me?"

"No, not specially. Do you like Karen's?"

"*Do* I!"

"Did you ever lay Karen?"

"You know damn well I didn't."

"Did you ever make a pass at her?"

"Often."

"Do you want to lay her?"

"Do you want an honest answer?"

"If I asked her to, as a favor to me, she would, I think."

"What would you say to her?"

"I'd say I had the curse or I was pregnant or whatever it happened to be, and I didn't want you to go around

with other women and get a disease. Or I'd just *say* to her,
Jim wants to sleep with you and I want him to have what
he wants, and she'd do it. I think she would."

"I'm not so sure. Sometimes I think she doesn't like
me."

"Yes, she does. I think she'd like to sleep with you. She
asked me one time how you were in bed. She's very curious about it. She never had an orgasm with a man. Something always goes wrong."

"She's never been in love," I said. "She'd be all right if
she'd fall for some guy and have a long affair with him.
She's a perfectly normal girl, and with the right guy."

"That's the great difficulty. I think you might be the
right guy."

"Don't put ideas in my head. Your father certainly
thinks—"

"He's horrible. He was trying to put his hand up her
skirt all last Saturday night. He wanted me to ask her to
spend the night with us, and I almost did but something
stopped me. I wish he'd go away and never come back. I
wish he'd never come here in the first place. Still, I guess
I always would have been curious about him. Wanting
to know what he looked like, and whether he was alive.
Well, I know now."

"By the way," I said.

"I didn't find out anything. He carries a pistol. I found
that out."

"How?"

"I saw it in his back pocket when he was coming out of
the bathroom."

"Did he know you saw it?"

"No, I don't think he did. He didn't try to hide it,
though."

"Has he said how long he's going to stay?"

"No. I didn't know how to broach the subject. I know
he'll be here till after Christmas."

"Well, that's not very long. What does he do in the
daytime?"

"Well, of course I'm never there, so I don't really know.

He's home for lunch usually, Millie tells me. He gets up
after I've gone to the shop and goes out and comes back
with the Chicago and New York papers. Oh, yes. He buys
racing papers. I imagine he must play the horses quite a
lot."

"Good God, you don't think he's going to be here for
the whole Santa Anita meeting?"

"God forbid! But I wonder why he carries a pistol.
Maybe he is a detective."

"Well, let's us be detectives. Does he get any phone calls
at the house?"

"Not that I know of."

"Mail?"

"Well, yes, but not at the house. General Delivery, I
think."

"Doesn't he ever try to explain what he's doing out
here?" I said. "I should think he'd feel that he had to say
something about his plans."

"No. He sometimes gives me the impression that he
thinks this is his home. Our house. And he's the father,
and we're the children. Goodness knows I never have any
such feeling."

"I guess we'll just have to wait and see," I said. I
turned over and we lightly kissed each other and felt our
passion slowly coming on again. "Ah, this is nice. This is
what we're here for, isn't it?"

"Mm-hmm. Want me to stay all night?"

"Sure. It's a long time since we've done that."

"After a while I'll call Millie and tell her I'm not coming home, and I'll fix it with Karen. I want to stay in your
nice new house, but let's sleep in the room with the double bed. Not now, but when we go to bed tonight."

"Anything you say. I'd like to christen every room in
the house."

"In one night? Not if I know you. Am I good for you,
Jim?"

"Yes, you're good for me. Am I good for you?"

"Yes. Yes," she said. "Yes. Yes!"

10

I HAD a friend, not exactly a friend, but a fellow I had known slightly in New York, although I had known him well by reputation. He was a hard one to figure out. He did a little tap-dancing in the Guinan days, and he was what we call around-Broadway. He had been a press agent, hoofer, errand boy for gamblers, and more than once I had seen him getting a nod from big shot public enemies. I seriously doubt whether he ever was convicted of major crime, or even was accused of it. He was not hopheaded enough or ruthless enough to be a torpedo. In fact, I am not even sure that he would actually steal, although he often referred to himself as "a larceny guy like me." This probably was his euphemism for chiseller. He was a chiseller, all right, but I liked him. He had come to Hollywood around 1930 or '31, as a "technical advisor" on a gangster picture. He appeared in the picture, and in several subsequent ones. Then he was an artists' representative for a while, and after that he sold an original story, based on fact. "I made a little," he was always saying, to cover his business activities.

He wrote and acted under the name of Jerry Luck, but everybody called him Red; I don't know why. I telephoned him from the studio the day after Peggy and I housewarmed. I made a date for breakfast, or lunch. We met at the Beverly Derby. He had not gone Hollywood in his clothes. He had on a one-button suit of Eleanor Blue, black pointed shoes with Spanish heels to give him a little extra height, soft white shirt that had been

starched too much, and a spotless, almost white hat. He
was carrying one of those wrap-around camel's-hair coats.
When I got there, he said, "Jim boy," without looking at
me. "Don't turn round now, but ain't that that Loretta
Young?"

"Mm—yes," I said.

"That's for me," he said. "Where do we sit?"

We got a table. He carefully folded his coat, carefully
laid down his hat, and smoothing his suit coat over his
hips, he sat down, taking in the whole room slowly. He
picked up the menu and read it item by item, and then
tossed it in front of him like a disgusted cardplayer. "Frig
dat," he said. "Hey! Miss!" he called the waitress.

She said hello to me, and gave him her attention. "Yes,
sir?"

"You wanna go in pictures?" he said.

"Sure," she said.

"All right then, get this order and I and Mr. Malloy
may have a part for you in our next picture. I want—"
and he held out his hands like a man holding a water-
melon. "I want some of that brannis wit' the portis salad
dressing on top wit' a little—Jim, what's the name of that
sauce?"

"Escoffier?" I said.

"Escoffyer sauce. You know?"

"I'm sorry, sir, I didn't get it," she said.

"She didn't get it," he said. "All right, once again. Now
look. I want some of this brancovy portis like wit' the
cullaba on *top! On top!* Usely you don't put it on top
here, but that's the way I want it—"

"I'm sorry, sir—"

"You're sorry! Jesus Christ, she's sorry. What am I,
talkin' Greek or Saskatchewan or sumpn? Calla head
waiter. Calla captain." The poor girl brought the captain.

"You the captain?"

"Yes, sir."

"I'm S. J. Sterncliff from Gaumont British. Y'ever hear
Gaumont British?"

"Oh, yes, sir," said the captain.

"Well, that's who I am, the New York representative Gaumont British. Now this here is my first trip to Hollywood and I'm accustomed to the best, the best. I ask this young lady to bring me a brannis salad wit' the portis on top like wit' the Escoffyer. You.know."

The captain looked at me and smiled sadly, and then at Red. "Is this the double talk, sir?"

"Oh, a wise guy. Okay. Gimme a bacon and tomato on whole wheat toasted. Coffee. Wudda *you* eatin', Jim boy?"

I ordered corn beef hash. The captain and the girl left us.

"To what do I owe this honor, Kiddy?" said Red.

"A favor, Red," I said. "Do you know any private dicks?"

"Do I! You mean them gumshoe artists, Jim? Those hawkshaws? Those flatfoots, Jim?"

"Yes."

"Indeed I do. They have shadowed and tailed me all over the length and breadth of this fair land. Are you leveling? Why do you ask?"

"I'm leveling. Did you ever know one by the name of Henderson?"

"Henderson. No, not by that name. Why?"

"How's your memory for faces?"

"The best, Jim. A second Al Smith. A *first* Al Smith. A veritable photographic memory, if you know what I mean, Jim."

"I have a guy I want you to take a gander at."

"You mean give him the double-O, Jim? The onceover? The up and down, Jim?"

"Yes."

"Done, sir, done. You have my hand on it, and when a Luckman gives his hand, you better go right to Doctor Wharton, one flight up, leave this place as you find it. Is it you, or somebody else?"

"It's somebody else. A couple of other people, in fact," I said.

"What can I do? You want me to look at this guy and see if I know him."

"Right."

"Where is he, Jim?"

"I'll find out right away, if I can." I had a phone brought to the table, and called Peggy. She happened to be at the bookstore, and I told her to call her home and see if her father was there. I had a plan. She called me back and said he was there.

"If you're not doing anything for the next half hour," I said.

"All afternoon, Jim. Anything you say. Jesus, that Loretta Young. Who's that with her?"

"Eddie Sutherland. You know him."

"Eddie Sutherland the director. No, I don't know him. He was at Paramount when I was there a couple times."

"He's *still* there," I said.

"All right, pallie, you don't have to put salt in the wound. Here she comes."

"Hello, Eddie," I said. "Hello, Gretch. Gretch, this is Mr. Luck, Miss Young. Mr. Sutherland." Red did a scramble like Benchley in How To Behave, and they passed on. Red grabbed my arm.

"Pardon the vise-like grip," he said, "but anything you want, Jim. Anything you want. Anything she wants, too. A ray of sunshine in a drab life. A merciful angel. A lady bountiful whose very smile."

"I didn't know you cared, Red."

"Cared! For the pal who introduced me to Loretta Young—anything! Where is this Henderson? I will bring together the mains and the semi-mains and we will put the son of a bitch on the spot, Jim. We will rub him out. His number is up. We will *see* him, Jim. You know the sinister meaning of see, don't you?"

"Yes, dear," I said.

"You sure you don't want me to stop for my chopper? My typewriter? My tommy-gun, Jim? We'll let him have it, the rat."

"Just the double-O is all I want, Red," I said. "And the check, honey. Bobbie. Naomi. Betty. Ella. Check, please?"

My plan was simple. We would go to Peggy's house and pretend I had a date to meet her there. We would stay long enough for Red to get a good look at Henderson, and then retire. This we did.

Henderson was home. Millie came to the door and I motioned to her to let us in. "Is Peggy home yet?" I said, pretty loud.

"No, Mist' Malloy, she ain't home yet. Won't *be* home before six I guess."

"Yes, she was coming home. I was to meet her here."

"Well, in that case I guess you better come in wait. Will you rest your hats?"

"Ah, Malloy," said Henderson. "This is quite a surprise."

"I was supposed to meet Peggy here around two-thirty. Didn't she phone or anything?"

"Only to tell Millie what to have for dinner. About I'd say a half an hour ago."

"This is Mr. Luck, Mr. Henderson."

"Glad to meet you."

"Glad to meet *you*."

"It's funny she didn't call. She's usually pretty uh punctilious," I said.

"Why don't you try calling her at the store?" said Henderson. "Sit down, Mr. Lock?"

"Luck."

"Luck. Anything in the name, eh?" said Henderson.

"Lots of it. All bad," said Red.

I telephoned, putting on my act for Henderson's benefit. "She says she forgot all about it," I said. "Well—"

We left. On the way down the hill in my car Red was biting his lower lip. "We can go to the Bamboo Room and refresh your memory."

"That won't do any good," he said. "Of course we can *go*. I'll buy a powder."

We sat down in the too-low chairs of the Bamboo Room.

"I'll tell you the God's honest truth," said Red. "I don't know."

"Well, it was only a chance," I said. "One in a million."

"No, it's better than that," he said. "When we first got there I was positive I never saw him before in my whole life but while you was at the phone I kept looking at that kisser and, I don't *know*. You don't know if he took on weight or something? He couldn't of taken on *much*, but maybe just enough."

"Were you ever in Chicago?"

"A million times."

"For any length of time?" I asked.

"A week, two weeks. Split weeks in the neighborhood houses. I was to open in a club there once. I'm sorry, Jim. I'd like to straighten you out on this, but I honestly can't. I can't swear I ever saw him before, and I can't swear I didn't."

"When you were around the clubs did you ever meet a guy that sold silverware, knives and forks?"

"No, I wouldn't of been around doorn that phase. Of course a guy like that would come back and spend a little if he sold the silverware to the club."

"That's what I was thinking."

"Yeah. But that's no clue. I just have to give up till I can go to work on the old memory."

"Red. A personal question, and you don't have to answer it. Did you ever do time?"

"Yes," he said. "But he didn't. I'd bet on that."

"Thanks, pal," I said. "You're pretty sure?"

"Well, you can always be wrong about that. You hear about these guys that take a powder from some chain gang and they go and live in Ohio or some place and veil up and live respectable lives for fifteen years and nobody the wiser. But most of the time it's like the clap. I can tell you in this room who had the clap. You did, didn't you?"

"Sure."

"That guinzo over there. He had it. I had it, and I can tell just by lookin' at a guy. Usely I can wit' guys that did time, and I would say this Henderson never did. Jim, I'd like to be able to say I made that guy the minute I laid eyes on him, but I can't say that. If I did I'd be telling you a lie. But one thing I will say."

"What's that?"

"This much I will say. If I ever saw a wronggo, that Henderson is it."

"I'll go with you on that," I said.

So we sat and had a few powders and I got my load on and had to have Jonas come down in a taxi and take me home, as I never drive when I am a little stiff.

11

CHRISTMAS stank. Maybe it is because I am a sucker for Christmas, and this was my first in Hollywood. Always before I had gone East, or happened to be East. It doesn't have to be White for me to like it, but it ought to be reasonably cold, and there never ought to be palm trees. Well, maybe palm trees. I could easily have made a better day of it in the Gauguin country, me in torn shorts and the girls in sarongs or better, and all of us drinking out of coconuts. As it was I took the day off on Christmas Eve and went around buying presents. I bought Keith a $25 shockproof wristwatch. I bought Karen a metal vanity case that looked like a radio set and weighed about two pounds, and cost $80. I bought Red a pigskin cigarette case for $15. I sent Millie a telegraph money order for $10 because I was sure she'd never had one before. I gave Jonas and his wife two weeks' pay, and I bought toys for the children of people who have no part in this story. I was glad to get a tie from Don Miller, sent to the studio. And I put down $400 on a star sapphire ring for Peggy. I had everything sent, except the ring, and then I went to a party at the studio and then a cocktail party at somebody's house and then had Jonas drive me to the bookstore to pick up Peggy. She would have kept me waiting, but that was all right, because I went to the bar at the Beverly-Wilshire and plied myself with Scotch and soda, humming the praises of good King Wenceslaus with a dash of Lord Jeffrey Amherst and I'm Only a Mercersburg Boy, which was to make me homesick. I got very drunk and they asked me to leave. I went across the street to the Brown Derby and distributed largesse of five dollars to each waitress except my favorite, to whom I gave $4.49. I told her if she was a good girl for the rest of the year I would give her the rest. I felt very good, but that was Christmas Eve.

Peggy was sitting in the car. I got in and took her hand and kissed it. "I have whiskey on my breath," I said.

"On your *breath!*"

"I've tried Sen-Sens and cloves, but no good. Now this little hand, which I now kiss, kiss, indicating kiss on hand, have you got a kiss on hand, Miss? I'll take—anyway. This little hand which I now kiss, I now decorate like gilding the lily." Then I put the ring on her thumb. "It doesn't mean anything unless you want it to, so put it whatever finger your heart's desire."

She took it off and looked at it and at me, and put it on the third finger of her left hand. "I don't care," she said. "Even if you are drunk." She put her arms around my neck and kissed me, and I started to cry because I loved her.

"I gotta cut this out," I said. "You like my house I bought for you?"

"You didn't buy it," she said.

"All right, I didn't buy it. All right. Very well. I didn't buy the God damn thing. I guess I didn't buy it, eh? Jonas!"

"Yes, sir."

"Have you got the deed of our house in your pocket? Do you happen to have it?"

"No, sir."

"Hmm. Well, maybe you're right, then. I didn't buy it. But I will. If you like it, that is. Contingent on your liking it only. Otherwise—the hell with it. We'll go set fire to the God damn thing. Let's do it anyway. Only fooling. Firemen are all drunk on Christmas Eve, drunk and home with their wives and little children."

"Will you take me home now?"

"Don't you want to go to our little home?"

"I want to go to my own little home. *Next* Christmas we'll go to our little home, and we'll have little children like the firemen."

"I can't have little children. Only big little children. We'll go to the Shelter and adopt two big little children and get a lot of publicity, like the movie stars. Wonderful, kind movie stars, adopting poor little waifs. Waives? Waifs. We get our picture in the paper. Mr. and Mrs. James Malloy with the poor little kiddies they adopted out of the kindness of their hearts because Mr. and Mrs. Malloy are so big-hearted. Especially Mrs. Malloy. Darling, I hope you don't mind being Mrs. Malloy? There's another one around somewhere."

"I know."

"Do you mind?"

"Sure I mind, but what can I do about it?"

"Maybe she'll marry somebody and then she won't be Mrs. Malloy. Maybe she'll marry the Duke of Windsor. At long last I'm gonna say a few God damn words of my own, you sons of bitches. Maybe she'll marry Oswald Mosley."

"Who? Mrs. Simpson?"

"Mrs. Malloy. I'm a great lover of music, Peggy."

"I know."

"Adeste fideles, laeti triumphantes. Venite, venite in Beth-le-hem. I used to be a boy tenor. At SS. Peter and Paul."

"SS. Peter and Paul sounds more like a ship."

"That reminds me. Jonas, you know where Miss Henderson lives? Well, start tacking, Jonas. That's where we're going. Everybody's tackin'. They hadda have something new. Tacking. I love all music, Peggy. You know that, don't you?"

"Yes."

"You know I love you, too, don't you, Peggy?"

"Yes."

"Do you know that?"

"Yes, I guess so."

"That's right. At least I love you as much as I can love anybody that isn't James Malloy. I hate him."

"I'm James Malloy, too."

"What?"

"I said I'm James Malloy, too."

"God knows I hope you mean what I think you do."

"I do."

"Kiss me."

"All right." She kissed me. "I think I'd like to get a little tight, too."

"I don't blame you. I always get nervous when I'm sober and someone's tight and I'm with them. But you gotta go some, my sweet."

We stopped at the Trocadero and there was hardly anyone there. We had Lanson 1926. "Drink up, sweet. You gotta go some. How I love music. Frère Jacques, Cuernavaca, ach du lieber August. All languages. A walking Berlitz. Berlitz sounds like you with that champagne, my sweet, or how you're gonna sound." We drank a quart of champagne and Peggy began to get a little tight.

"Waiter!" I called. The waiter came.

"There's a drunken man," I said.

"Where, sir?" he said.

"Here. Me," I said.

"Yes, sir."

"Oh, yeah? You wanna make sumpn of it? Where's Billy Wilkerson?"

"He isn't here, sir."

"If this place is good enough for me it's good enough for him. Let's get outa here, Peggy."

"All right. I'm willing. Woo-woo!" We left, both saying woo-woo quietly.

Jonas had the car parked on Sunset instead of on the parking lot, which was a good thing. We got in, and Peggy leaned forward. "Jonas," she said.

"Yes, Miss Henderson."

"The stockings were hung by the chimney with care. Finish it."

"In hopes that St. Nicholas soon would be there," said Jonas.

"Woo-woo," said Peggy.

"None of your lip," I said. "Yes. Some of your lip."

"Merry Christmas, cried the warden, and the prisoners shouted balls."

"Woo-woo. I drank that fast too champagne," said Peggy. "Woo-woo."

"Whose little home shall we go to?" I said. "Let's go to the Bide-a-Wee Home. The Ellin Speyer Home."

"Let's go to the Wee Kirk o' the Heather. Who is Ellin Speyer?"

"Ellin Prince Speyer? You don't know her? You must be drunk. I'll take you home and put you to bed."

"Aw, now you're hinting," said Peggy. She tried to whistle.

"How're you ever gonna wet your whistle, when the whole darn world goes dry? You're too young for that. Sahara, we sympathize with you, Sahara, we'll soon be dry like you. You're too young for that, too. How dark and still tonight, by the old distillery. I'm a different generation, Peggy. I'm too God damn old for you."

"Woo-woo."

"I am."

"Woo-woo."

"All you can think of is woo-woo."

"Woo-woo."

"Home, Jonas," I said.

"Woo-woo. No. My home."

"Stop at the Seven Seas, Jonas." We drove to the Seven Seas, and we were the only people there. We had more champagne. The waiters stood around trying to smile, now and then slapping imaginary dust off the table-cloths. "Are you my baby?"

"Yes."

"Bore a hole, bore a hole—"

"Stop it! I've changed. I'm dignified now."

"I like to think of old Bethlehem, tonight. Yes, I like to

think of old Bethlehem. And old Allentown, and old
Easton. And Catasauqua."

"I don't." Then suddenly: "I've got to go home. Come
on."

Jonas drove us to her house. We sang on the way, and
necked while we sang. She hummed Some Day I'll Find
You, and I simply repeated, neeah-neeah, neeah-neeah.
Outside her house she said: "How do you like my new
ring that some man gave me for Christmas?"

"Well—ostentatious. I hope he does right by you. Who
is the guy? A girl doesn't get a ring like that for nothing."

"He is my betrothed. I want you to be the first to
know," she said. "Are you sure you want me to have it?"

"Well, temporarily. In about twenty years we'll wake
up some day and realize it was only sex."

"Come in for a minute," she said.

We went in and Henderson was reading the paper.
"Oh, there you are. Malloy. Say, are you drunk? Peggy?"

"Not very. Just a little."

"Now look here, Malloy. She's a young girl."

"She's twenty-one," I said.

"Twenty-one? That's young. How old are you? You
must be thirty-five."

"Oh, for Christ sake."

"Did you wait supper?" said Peggy.

"I had mine. Keith just got home, too," said Henderson.

"I'll go tell Millie I'm home."

She staggered just a little and Henderson watched her.
"You wait," she said to me.

Henderson stood there with the paper in his hand.
"Malloy, I want to have a talk with you."

"Oh, for Christ sake."

"Yes, for Christ sake. We might as well have this out
now, unless you're too drunk."

"I'm not too drunk but there's nothing to have out.
You might as well get that straight."

"Oh, no? Where was Peggy last night?"

"At Karen's. Why?"

"That's a lie. I happen to know she wasn't at Karen's."

"Well, I happen to know she was. I took her there."

"Yeah? What time?"

"After work. Why? Are you implying she was with me?"

"Implying nothing. This is the second time she said she was at Karen's, and the other time I *know* she was with you."

"Listen, Henderson, it's a little late in the day for you to be coming around acting the stern parent."

"That goes for me, too," said Keith, in the doorway. He had a towel in his hand and was drying the inside of his ear.

"You. What kind of a brother *are* you? I guess you've known about this all along."

"Thanks for the watch, Jim. Cats, it was swell. I didn't get you anything but I just couldn't."

"Your money isn't wanted here, Malloy. I have enough to take care of my family."

"Aw, why don't you shut up?" said Keith.

"Now you listen here—" said Henderson, taking a step towards Keith.

"I wouldn't if I were you," I said. "He'll knock your block off."

"And you'd help him, I suppose."

"Gladly. But he wouldn't need my help. Listen, Henderson, why don't you get wise to yourself? These kids have got along without you for a long time. If you want to be a father you have to be it in a different way."

"I don't need any advice from you. I guess that's where they get their radical ideas from."

Peggy came in, apparently having gone from the kitchen to the bathroom which she shared with Keith. "I doused my face in cold water," she said. "Keith, look." She held out the ring finger.

"Cats! What is that?"

"Star sapphire. See it, Father?"

Henderson looked down and frowned, then looked at her and at me. Peggy came to me and pulled my head down and kissed me.

"Jim! Congratulations," said Keith, squeezing my
hand. He kissed Peggy, and Henderson shook hands with
me. "I'm sorry," he said, and then he held out his hand
and kissed Peggy's forehead. I think it was the first time
he had kissed her. Anyway, Peggy looked around at everybody, sat down on the sofa, and then quietly passed out.
We all laughed and Keith went to the kitchen and got
Millie to put her to bed. We had a few drinks and then I
left as soon as I could and went to a Christmas-tree-trim-
ming party out in Beverly, and Jonas got me home somehow.

12

I DID not go back to the studio until the Tuesday morning after Christmas, and when I did my stenographer
said someone had been calling me almost every hour in
my absence. That Tuesday afternoon she said I was
wanted on the phone, and she said she was sure it was the
same person who had been calling. Wouldn't give his
name. I told her to put him on.

"Malloy?"

"Yes."

"This is that friend of Pat's. Don't mention my name
if you recognize my voice."

"Yes. I know who it is."

"Will you do me another favor? This is a big one."

"What is it?"

"You know that place where I used to live?"

"Yes. I think so."

"That's all right, if you don't remember. I sent you a
telegram with just the address."

"Yeah."

"Well, this is the favor. Will you go there and there's
a fairy there that runs the switchboard. Blond-haired.
About my age. You go to him and ask him if there was
anybody there looking for me. Then I'll phone you tomorrow and you tell me. I can't call there myself because
they may have the wires tapped."

"That sounds pretty melodramatic," I said.

"Well, will you do it? I'm going nuts," said Miller. "If

there was anybody looking for me find out what he looks
like."

"All right. I'll go this afternoon, late," I said. "By the
way, thanks for the tie."

"Don't say that," he said. "Throw it away or they may
trace it."

"Jesus," I said. "You've got it bad."

That was all the conversation we had. In a few minutes
the telegram came, and late that afternoon I went to the
address he gave, a sort of hotel on Gower Street. They
called it a bachelors' club. You went up three steps and to
the left as you went in there was a door and a window on
one side of the hall. That was the office. The switchboard
was behind the window.

"May I help you?"

I looked down and there was this fairy with a sunlamp
tan and almost platinum blond, wavy hair. He was sitting
on a low chair behind the switchboard and he had to hold
his head back, chin up, to see me. With just a little nar-
rower face I swear he would have made a swell ad for
Tangee lipstick.

"I'm a friend of Mr. Miller's."

"Oh, Donnie's? How is he? You're the second person
asked for him today."

"Well, that's what I came about. Could you tell me
who else was looking for him?"

"The party didn't leave his name. Very mysterious. He
wanted to know all about Donnie. Of course I couldn't
tell him much."

"Oh, I'll bet you could."

"I *beg* your pardon?"

"Skip it. What about this guy. What'd he look like?"

"Well—he was about, ah, a man of forty, perhaps? Not
quite your height? With a nice head of hair for his age?
That is, not bald. Nice teeth?"

"How was he dressed?"

"Oh, very conservatively. Nothing flashy. The business
man type, you know?"

"Yes. What did he say?"

"Oh, just how long since I saw Donnie, and what did he look like. Oh, yes. He asked me if I ever cashed any checks for Donnie. Me cashing checks! Oh, I know who you must be. I've been wracking my brains. Are you Mr. Malloy?"

"Yes."

"I *thought* I recognized you from your picture. I loved your book. It was so true to life even if it was a fantasy. I mean I believed it all the time. I really did. I wish I had a copy here, I'd ask you to autograph it, but my friend went away and took it with him."

"Why the dirty thing," I said. "I'll send you one. What's your name?"

"Noel Sherman. Not Lowell Sherman. *Noel* Sherman."

"As in Noel Coward?"

"Yes, but it really is my name. My middle name," he said. "Will you really send me an autographed copy?"

"Of course I will. Noel Sherman. It's a pretty name. Well, thanks very much."

"Oh, notta tall, Mr. Malloy. Glad to oblige." He stood up and I left.

The next day Miller phoned and I told him Henderson was getting warm. That was the last I ever heard from Don Miller.

For the next week I was as industrious as I could be under the circumstances, they being an average of two parties a day at my friends' houses. It just seemed as though all my married friends decided that the Christmas-New Year's period was the time to give parties, and I wanted them all to meet Peggy. Not many of them knew her, because they mostly patronized a bookstore in Hollywood, not the Beverly one where Peggy worked. The women were nice to Peggy, and of course the men were too. They all wanted to know when we were going to get married, to which Peggy's answer was that we hadn't made up our minds, but soon, she said. I went around glowing, because it was a new thing to me. I was proud of Peggy and glad people liked her. I felt much older than Peggy, which of course I was; but I felt younger myself

than I had in years. Maybe ever. My other marriage had
not been very good, and there had been no engagement.
My first wife was rich and older than I and divorced, and
her friends used to make me feel like a God damn March-
banks, although I think I really loved her at the time. So
it was all new to me, and it was fun, and I guess it was
kind of fun for my friends, practically all of whom had
settled down at their homes and work and children and
some extra-marital dabbling. They were mostly newspaper men I had known in New York, and their first or
second wives, and all the men wrote or produced pictures.
There were only two movie actresses in the lot, and they
knew their place and were always trying to improve themselves, like reading books and going to concerts and buying Picassos and publicly smuggling contributions to the
I. L. D. I guess they were all right. Anyway the week
passed, and there was a lot of talk about giving parties for
Peggy. The parties never came off, because in the second
week of the new year Peggy's father killed Keith.

13

ON THE second Wednesday morning after New Year's
Peggy had gone to the shop early as it was her turn
to open it. Every other day she opened up, her boss doing
it on the alternate days. When she was leaving the house
she called to Keith to snap out of it and get to school, and
he called back to her that he was taking a couple of cuts
to go down to Vermont Avenue to the dentist. Her father
was not up yet when she left. (She had given notice at the
shop. I wanted to get married right away. She told her
boss, who always had been nice to her, that she would
look around for a good girl to take her place. Now I wish
she had quit right away.)

At about eleven-thirty that morning Millie telephoned
her and told her to come, that something terrible had
happened. Millie did not make much sense, and it took
all of Peggy's pleading to get Millie to tell her what kind
of terrible thing, and then Millie told her that her father
had shot her brother.

I am trying to give the straight facts on this first.

Peggy told her boss what little she knew, and he closed
the shop and they got into his car and at the corner of
Santa Monica and Rodeo they saw a motorcycle cop he
knew, and the cop gave them an escort out of Beverly,
then they got another somewhere along Sunset and were
at Peggy's house in less than fifteen minutes.

There were two police cars outside the house, and a
small group of people. Peggy and her boss went in, and
her father was sitting in the living-room with his head in

his hands, with two cops leaning against a bookcase, their caps on the back of their heads, and smoking. Henderson had no coat or vest on and his shirt was open.

Keith was not there. They had taken him to a hospital. Henderson looked up just once and said: "Don't ask me anything, Peggy. All I can say, it was an accident."

Peggy's boss picked out a nice cop and he went with them to the hospital. When they got there Keith was in the operating room, and Peggy had to wait. While she was waiting Karen's mother arrived at the hospital, and she waited with Peggy, and then before they brought Keith out of the operating room Karen arrived too.

The doctor in charge said it would be "some time" before Keith came out of the ether. He lied, and said Keith had about an even chance to live. He had lost a lot of blood, and there were internal hemorrhages besides. Then Peggy told Karen to phone me, but I was not in my office. I had gone to a projection room to watch a picture being run off, and after that I had gone to kill some time before lunch with Don McGinnis, a writer, whose office was nowhere near mine. I went off the lot for lunch, and did not get Karen's message until around three o'clock. I went straight to the hospital, but I did not see Peggy until around six-fifteen, five minutes after Keith died.

He recovered consciousness a little sooner than they expected. He opened his eyes, and when he did he was as conscious as you or I. A detective was there, and a doctor and two nurses and Peggy and Mrs. Waner. He said hello, faintly, and then the detective began to ask him questions, like, "Who fired the shot?" and "How'd it happen?" The poor kid knew he had to save breath, so he told the detective only two things: "It was an accident," and "It was my fault," and then he said to Peggy: "Right hand up, Peggy. My fault." Then he said hello to Karen and she started to cry, and a sort of bored look came into his eyes and he made that noise in his throat and died. Peggy looked at him for a minute and then she heard the doctor say to the detective: "Remarkable. Seven hours. Why do you know, that bullet—" That was when she came out.

She came right to me as though she had known exactly where I would be, and she took my arm. I thank God I had sense enough not to try to say anything. Then I saw a cop coming out of the room and I asked him if it would be all right for me to take Miss Henderson home, and he asked the detective, who said he saw no reason why not. Peggy's boss came up to her and said: "Miss Henderson, anything I can do. If you want money, or anything. I'd consider it a privilege."

"Thank you, Mr. Milton," she said. "I'll let you know." Then she pressed my arm and we walked to the elevator and went out and got in my car.

I offered her a cigarette, and she took it, and the lighter wouldn't work. I reached for matches, but she said she didn't really want to smoke. She looked at me a couple of times. She wanted to tell from the expression on my face how she was taking it, or how I thought she was taking it. A cop came up and told me he'd have to give me a ticket if we didn't move on, and I showed him an honorary detective's badge that I had borrowed from Don McGinnis. "Well, don't stay too long," he said. "They blame me if this place ain't clear."

"Let's drive up to the top of the mountain," Peggy said. We drove up, high above the broken Hollywoodland sign, and she took off her hat and rested the back of her head on the leather seat. Her hands were in her lap. Her pretty legs were stretched out straight under the dash. I sat and looked at her, and I wanted to kiss her, but I didn't. It was so quiet that I could hear the tiny sound as she moistened her dry lips.

"How does it feel to be a Catholic?" she said.

"Sometimes good, sometimes bad."

"Do Catholics believe that when you die your soul goes up in the sky? To heaven, if they go to heaven?"

"The poor people do. The educated ones believe that heaven is a state, a sort of metaphysical state. At least I think that's right."

"The soul doesn't rise, up in the air?"

"No."

She waited. "That was one of the reasons why I wanted to come up here. If *you* believed that, about their going up in the air, you'd be close to him. I don't believe it, but if you did I wanted to be with you while you believed it. Now I can never be a Catholic. The only thing I ever wanted from the Catholic Church I can't have. One little thing. But I guess he'll be just as alive down there, home. Oh, God! Oh, Jesus! He will be, Jim!" Then she broke, and so did I.

She stopped crying before I did, and this time she lit a cigarette and told me all she knew, starting by saying: "I have to be practical now. He said my father didn't do it on purpose, and I believe him. I wouldn't believe him, but now I remember how my father looked when I got home. I wouldn't have believed him, because he would have lied. That's the way he was. Look how soon it's the past tense. He was." She puffed on her cigarette. "What will they do?"

"They'll hold him, your father. Probably for manslaughter. I think probably involuntary manslaughter, if he has anything like an explanation. A lot depends on you, maybe a little on me, and a lot on Millie. If they knew Keith didn't like your father, he'd have a tough time. What do you want to do?"

"I want him to go away so I'll never see him again."

"Well, then I guess—I wish we knew what Millie told the cops. We can take a chance on repudiating what Millie might say. Hysterical colored woman saying anything in a crisis." I thought a minute. "I know one thing you can do."

"What's that?"

"You can say you're going to get a lawyer for your father. I'll give you the money. Then when they ask around they'll find out how much you loved Keith, so they won't think—I have to be blunt, Peggy."

"I know."

"Well, they won't think you were, oh, relieved by Keith's death. See what I mean? You're the loving sister, but you're also the loving daughter, convinced that it was accidental. I know a hell of a good lawyer in Pasadena. He doesn't try criminal cases, but he'll know the best one to get. I'll call him right away as soon as we leave here. By that time they'll have taken your father downtown and booked him. They won't let him out on bail. At least for a while. Depends on what they decide to do. This is a good time of year, you know."

"Why?"

"Well, no election going on or coming up. When there's an election coming up the D. A. tries to get as many convictions as he can to make him look good. If your father has a good defense, they're likely to figure on saving the expense of a trial. I'll do all I can."

"I know you will," she said. "All I want is to get him away from here and never come back."

I took my arm away from her and put my hands on the wheel. "What about us? You're alone, now. Let's get married as soon as we can."

"There's no hurry, is there?" she said. "Either way."

"What do you mean, either way?"

"Well, I don't know. There's no hurry."

14

We did it as we planned, and it came out as we wanted it to. I telephoned my Pasadena friend, and he made a good suggestion: not to get the local Leibowitz, but to get a less conspicuous but able lawyer for Henderson. The idea being that the Fallons and the Rogerses often get a case tried by the newspaper reporters before the suspect is indicted. People think the suspect is guilty because he hires the top lawyer.

They booked Henderson on suspicion of murder, but that was as far as it got. The detectives had to make a report that favored Henderson, and the Coroner's jury report that followed gave a verdict of accidental death, and so the complaint deputy in the D. A.'s office refused to issue a complaint. The only worry, Millie, was out of the picture, because she was not in the house when the shooting occurred. She was five blocks away, at a market. Peggy, acting the loving daughter, was convincing. They asked me a few questions, but they didn't pay much attention to anything I said.

It was a one-day story in the papers, and not a very good one. The father was a private detective for a surety company, and had a permit for the .38 detective special, not in California, it was true, but in New York, where the Sullivan Law is tough about carrying revolvers. This information must have interested Don Miller, because there was a picture of Henderson on an inside page of the *Herald-Express,* and one enterprising reporter wrote that Henderson was in California in connection with some stolen traveler's checks. This information cost Henderson his job.

He was released in less than a week after Keith was killed, and he aroused no suspicion by making preparations to leave. I never knew whether he made the decision unaided, or if Peggy told him to go away.

The day before he left he came out to see me at the studio.

I did not get up when the stenographer led him in. She knew who he was, and she could hardly take her eyes off him. For her benefit I was cordial to him, and then I got up and closed the door.

"Cigarette?" he said.

"I have some," I said.

"I guess you know I lost my job," he said.

"Peggy told me."

"I'm going away," he said.

"I know. When?"

"Tomorrow. I'm going up to San Francisco. I figure it's better not to leave the state. I used to know a couple fellows in the Army. I might be able to get something up there."

"Probably."

"Malloy," he said, "you're making it tough for me. I guess I know what you think. You're thinking, here's a man that killed his own son, the brother of the girl I'm going to marry. I guess you wish I'd get the hell out of here, the way Peggy can't stand the sight of me. Can anybody hear me?"

"Not if you don't talk too loud."

"Malloy, I'm a young man, comparatively. Or I was. Now I'm an old man. I'm not looking for any sympathy. Most of my life I've been a louse, a bastard. Some of the time I had a good time, sometimes not. I was kicked out of college for something I didn't do. I have a letter somewhere to prove it. My own fraternity brothers thought I stole a gold watch and chain, and they asked me to hand in my pin. I did, and I was so surprised I didn't make any stink about it, so they believed I was guilty and I was kicked out. Then five or six months later they caught the guy that did it red-handed, and they wrote me a letter and sent me my pin. Here it is. But by that time I didn't give a God damn. I was one of those fellows, give a dog a bad name, and by that time I was living off a whore in Binghamton, New York.

"Well, I've been a lot of things in my time. I was indicted twice, money matters, but they could never make it stick, so I never did time. Then I've been in legitimate business several times and twice in my life I've had a credit rating of over a hundred thousand dollars. But I don't know, I knew a dame one time that was pretty good at fortune-telling. Palmistry. She looked at my hand and she said she wouldn't tell me what she saw. I'll bet she'd feel pleased with herself right now.

"Anyway, one thing, I've always been pretty good at sizing up people, and I became a private detective, because I can get to know people easily, and I never forget a face. And, I'm a good liar. Convincing. But you know I'm telling you the truth. For instance, I was within a week of catching up with your friend Schumacher, alias Donald R. Miller. Now I have no job, which is a break for him. Probably for you, too, but that's not what I came to tell you about. You know what I came here for?"

"Money?"

"No. I'll take some if you give it to me, but I don't give a f—— if you offer it to me or not. I came here, Malloy, because you're going to marry my daughter. As bad a father as I've been, she's my own flesh and blood and I'm proud of her. Maybe she wouldn't have been as good as she is if she'd had the kind of breaks she deserves. Her mother was—well, her mother was all right, too.

"What I came here for. The whole world knows I killed my own son, but I'm the only one in the world knows how it happened. I'm going to tell you so you can tell Peggy some time, whether you like it or not. And it's the truth.

"The morning he was killed he came in my room and I was getting dressed. I had my gun on the bureau and I was tying my tie when he came in my room. He stood there and looked at me a minute, and I said, 'What is it, son?' And he called me a son of a bitch or bastard or something, and I asked him what was the matter? Then he yelled at me 'God damn you,' he said, 'if you ever put a finger on Karen Waner again, I'll kill you.'

"Well, I pretended I didn't know what he was talking about, but I knew. The night before I had a date with this Waner kid. I met her down there at Third and Rossmore. She came down there in a taxi and she got in the car I had and we drove to Long Beach. We had a lot of drinks. On the way back I lost my way, and it wasn't any gag. I was lost. We ended up near the oil wells. Well, I made a pass at her and I thought she liked it. Hell's bells, she was willing to go out with me without letting anyone know it, and I figured what I figured. What anybody'd figure under the circumstances. I was her friend's father and she looked like the most beautiful piece of tail—well, anyway, the first thing I knew she was fighting me off. I thought that was put on, but she kept it up so I started the car and we came back to Hollywood. I guess I tore her dress.

"The next morning she must have been afraid Peggy'd find out or something like that, because she called up and Keith took the call, and what she told him I'll never know, but he must have sat there a while, burning, and I guess he liked her more than he ever let on. Be that as it may, he came in and the way I told you, called me a bastard and I told him to calm down, and then he got up. Well, at that very minute I happened to have my gun in my hand, putting it in my hip pocket. It was a detective special, which is a very dangerous thing to fool with. The next thing to hair trigger, this was, and a .38. Short barrel. You probably know what they're like."

"Sure."

"I had it in my hand, and I was looking at myself in the mirror, when he grabbed my arm. The gun went off, and got him right here. I don't see how it didn't kill him right away. Instantly. I'm glad it didn't, though, because he knows what I said to him when he fell on the floor. That's between him and me, but I think the kid knew it was an accident. I sound like a heel to say it, but it was his own fault. He said so on his deathbed. I think for the first time he knew that no matter how much of a louse I was, I wanted to change. But with a guy like me, the life I led, these changes don't come all of a sudden." He stopped. "Or *maybe* they do, Malloy. Maybe they do. In the last week I've changed. I don't know.

"Well, there it is, there's the story. You be good to Peggy, and sometime the time may come when you can tell her what I just told you. I'll never bother you or her. I'm disgusted."

I waited for him to say something more, but he didn't. He started to get up. He reached for his hat.

"Would five hundred bucks help you?" I said.

"One hundred bucks would help me."

"I'll let you have five," I said.

"You'll never get it back," he said.

"I know," I said. I started to write the check. "Henderson, I think I believe you."

"I don't *give* a damn any more. I've told you the truth."

"I'll give you the address of my agent. If you get in a bad jam, I mean you're badly on the nut or something like that, you write me care of this guy, and I'll let you have some more. On one condition."

"That I never bother Peggy. Don't worry. And thanks for the offer, but I'll never bother you, either. I don't think I will. If I do, don't send me any money. It'll only go for booze. That's what this is going for."

He had half a load on now, but was carrying it well.

"Here's your five. The bank in Beverly will cash it right away. They may call me, but that'll only take a minute."

"Thanks," he said. "Well, good luck." He looked at me and half smiled. He picked up the check, which I had laid on the desk in front of him. "You wouldn't even hand it to me, would you?"

"Nope."

"Well, take care of Peggy," he said. "Good-by, Mr. Malloy." And he left.

15

Peggy stayed in the little house for about a month after her father left, and during that time I saw her nearly every night. We went to the movies a few times, but one night on the way from the theater to the car she said she couldn't help thinking that the way a shot sounded in the picture must have been the way the shot sounded when Keith was killed. After that we stayed away from the movies. Instead we would go for long rides, long conversationless rides to Pomona and Santa Barbara, or nearer places when we had less time. Then we formed another habit, that of going to a late spot that I knew of, where the fellows from the dance orchestras would meet after work and have jam sessions. Nobody knew Peggy. Nobody wanted to. The life of the place was the jam session, and non-musicians went there under sufferance. I kept my own liquor there, and it was a good place for us, because Peggy had been developing a fondness for brandy.

During that month or so I expected, and observed, changes in Peggy, just as anyone would have. Her drinking, for instance. It had become a serious matter with her, almost a job. She always had been one to take a drink, but she had given it a holiday spirit. Now she had become a drinker. Well, she was a healthy girl, and she could take it; never got mean or noisy. I drink too fast myself, but now she was taking drink for drink with me. I didn't like it, but I never said anything, because she would have tried to explain what needed no explaining.

Herbert often phoned her, but I don't think she saw

him, unless he came to the shop (she wisely went back to work almost immediately). Otherwise she saw only Karen and me. One night as that first month was ending I suggested dinner at my house, and she said all right. It was the first time she had been there since Keith was killed. Jonas and his wife turned out a good dinner, and after dinner we sat in the library, a small room with sets of books and tennis trophies that had been left behind by the owner of the house. There was a Capehart in the room, and I put on some records and we sat and drank Courvoisier until about ten-thirty or so.

"Turn that thing down," she said. "Or turn it off altogether." I turned it off.

When I came back to the sofa, she said: "Jim, I know what you're going to say in a little while."

"Do you?"

"Yes. I'm sorry, Jim," she said, and held out her hand and I saw the star sapphire was in it.

"Oh," I said. I stood up and walked to the other side of the room and sat on an uncomfortable straight chair. "I don't suppose you'd have any reasons."

"You know the reasons," she said.

"Do I?" I said. "Well, anyway, keep the ring."

"No, you take it."

"No. When I gave it to you I put it up to you where you wanted to wear it. It was a Christmas present. So you keep it."

"All right. Thanks. You can always have it back. Do you want to take me home now?"

"Not unless you want to go."

"I don't, but I thought you might want me to."

"No," I said. We had a lot more to drink, and then we had a messy scene that I am ashamed of, and she made me take her home. I telephoned her the following night, but she told me she had a date with Herbert. After that I called her twice, late at night, when I was drunk and afraid, but she would not see me, and the next time I felt like that I remembered Charlotte, whom I had not seen since the night she was with Miller. Charlotte is all right.

Then my contract was expiring at Metro and there was some talk of a play of mine being produced in New York, and I was getting ready to leave, so I went to the shop to say good-by to Peggy. She was glad to see me. She started to smile when she saw me, and she kept smiling as she came up from the rear of the shop. "I hear good news about you," she said.

"About me?"

"The play. Congratulations. Is it the one I read last summer? Haven't they changed the title?"

"The title, and almost everything else," I said.

"Not the main idea, I hope. Remember I said I thought there were too many characters. When are you leaving?"

"Tuesday or Wednesday."

"Will you write to me?"

"What about, Peggy?"

"New York. The play. What you're doing."

"That's the kind of letter I'd write to Karen or somebody like that."

"You think I'm a heel, don't you?"

"No," I said.

"If I wrote to you, will you—no. You write to me and tell me where you're staying. I wanted to talk to you, but I think a letter would be better."

"Peggy, why don't you marry me and come with me? Are you in love?"

"I'd better write to you."

"Will you kiss me good-by?"

"Yes," she said. "Come to the back of the shop." We went to the back of the shop and I knew from the way she kissed me that she was not in love with someone else. I had a feeling at the time that she probably had not even kissed anyone else. "You must go now," she said. "Go on, Jim." I knew from the way she said it that she meant it and could not be made to change her mind.

The next I heard from her was when she wrote to me in New York. Here is the letter:

DEAR JIM:

I know now I never could have said what I have to say in a talk with you. The reason that I know it is that it is so hard to get started in a letter, without your distracting presence and equally distracting hands. With them I never could get started—if I ever do. (This makes the fifth attempt tonight.)

I love you, but as you have guessed and despite Francis Brett Young, love is not enough. It isn't even enough to know that not only do I love you, but that you also love me. I have known that since Christmas, but I did not entirely believe it until the day Keith died, when we went to the mountain. Since then, those first weeks, when you were kind and considerate and sensitive, I have wanted to do or say something to thank you, but when the time came at your house the same thing that kept me from telling you would not let me stay with you. The unreasonable aspect of that was that I wanted to stay with you, but here I am faced with the same suspicion, namely, that it wasn't only you I wanted to stay with. Almost anyone would have done. (Does this make any sense whatsoever?) Let me try again. Now don't go into a rage when I tell you this, but please read on and let me finish and then try to understand.

The whole trouble has been that you reminded me too much of my father, and at the same time you reminded me of Keith. I could not live with or sleep with that combination. All I wanted from you was the thing that you were giving me: peace, or silence in which to think. To return to your reminding me of my father, I do not mean physically (although your head is shaped like his). I refer to the way you *are*, the kind of life you have led, which in curious ways remind me of my father. You are not his generation, but you are not mine, either. You both have the same attitude toward life, which in a phrase is "To hell with it." At a time when I needed stability in someone, you gave me stability, and for that I was and am grateful, but, dear Jim, that could not last forever. I am not blaming you, but I think I was right in not seeing you because your dutiful stability was apt to exhaust itself while I still needed it. In one sense, it did. The night we had dinner at your house, the stability was beginning to crack, too soon. One more week might have made the difference, but I will not swear to that.

As to your reminding me of Keith, that is true too, but for an altogether different reason. When you are gay, you seem as young as Keith (and sometimes when you are not gay). If we were married, or if we had been married these past two months, the resemblance or things you have in common with Keith would have been unbearable. What I really want to say is that I have known so few men intimately that when one of the three men I have known intimately in the past six months, kills the man I loved best in the world, the third man is unfortunately identified with the other two. I grew to know my father and to think he had a certain charm. Then he killed Keith, and that left you, and somehow I resented you. I begin to realize that I have been resenting all men. If Herbert were not a sort of "cripple" as he calls himself, I could not stand him; but because of his poor health he is not a normal man, and another good thing about Herbert is that he will talk to anyone who will listen, which makes it very easy for me. He sits with me while I get tight, talking away, and never letting my glass become empty.

I have been sitting here since I finished the last paragraph, and I have come to the conclusion that it was a good thing to write this letter, despite the fact that it is not a good letter and does not say half of what I wanted to say. But it is making me think, and it is about time I did some straight thinking. I think if you were with me this minute we would be closer than at any time since Keith died, but I also think it is better that you are in New York. When you come back I will still be at the shop. My salary has been increased, and the boss is talking about taking a trip to Europe, leaving me in charge. Perhaps I will turn into an old-maid bookshop owner, an old maid with her memories. (But knowing myself, and knowing that inevitably you will return to Hollywood, I doubt that.) Be nice to the New York girls, but not too nice. I want you to be unattached when you come back here. Karen sends love and so do I, and I don't know which kind she means or which kind I mean. And write to me.

PEGGY.

16

M Y PLAY was an inconspicuous success, and I stayed
around New York half the summer, and then they
sold the play to the movies for $60,000 and I went back to
Hollywood for Universal. All I could think of on the
plane was that I was going to see Peggy, and how rich I
was. I did not tell her exactly when I would arrive. I
had written her "news" letters, and had had two news
letters from her. I arrived at the airport on a Sunday, just
before noon, and I telephoned her at home, at her new
apartment, but there was no answer. That night I saw her
at the Troc, and she was with my friend Don McGinnis
and two other people, all very tight. The next night I
had a date with her, and she stayed with me, but never
after that. She has not made up her mind about me, or
probably anything else. She goes to the Trocadero often,
but hardly ever more than two or three times with the
same man. I guess we are all washed up. Karen thinks so.

END.

The Fifty-Minute Hour

A BANTAM
SNEAK PREVIEW

by ROBERT LINDNER

"I am a psychoanalyst. I meet and work
with murderers, sadists, sex perverts—
people at the edge of violence—
and some who have passed that edge. These
are their stories as they told them
to me—searching, revealing, perhaps
shocking. But they are the raw
stuff of life itself, and therefore these people
are not beyond help.

—ROBERT LINDNER

Charles

If you had seen Charles on the street in your city, you would not have known him for a vicious killer. In prison, he still has a freshness of face that belongs in a choir stall. When I last saw him he was scarcely twenty-one. Even then, his eyes were blue and innocent, and he seemed to look at you with a perpetual questioning, as if to ask why a fence of steel must always stand between him and the trees he could see through the bars of his cell window.

Before Charles came to prison I had read about him in the newspapers. The case had made headlines for many days: it was composed of elements that were "naturals" for arousing public interest—a boy, a pretty girl—"Not so pretty," says Charles—an empty apartment, an ice-pick.

On a certain day in a certain city (according to the press) a young girl stood in the hallway of an apartment house. In one hand she carried a brief case with samples of religious books and records, in the other a purse and a portable phonograph. She hesitated before the panel of bells at the mailboxes, then rang one. There was no answer, so she rang a second, then a third, finally a fourth. At last a buzzer opened the lock of the inner door. She pushed against it with her shoulder and came into a narrow foyer with a staircase in the center. As she started up the steps, a youthful voice inquired who was there. Before she reached the first landing she saw a young man. He was standing by a partly opened door, looking at her. Recognizing by his youth that he could not be the head of this household, she smiled and asked if his mother were at home. He nodded, then waved his hand vaguely toward the interior of the apartment.

"She's in there," he said, and moved aside so she could pass.

"Can I see her?" she asked.

"Sure," he replied, "go on back. . . . She's in the bedroom."

The girl entered, turned to her left, and started down a passage. Midway, she passed a small kitchen. Near the door was an ice-box. On its porcelained top lay some tools. Ahead of her was the door to a bedroom. Just as she crossed the threshold she heard a noise behind her. She turned. As she did, the youth struck her on the head with a hammer. Then he stabbed her sixty-nine times with an ice-pick. Then he flung himself on the corpse . . .

WHAT MADE HIM KILL?

. . . and what drove an unhappy man into
Communism, or caused a young woman to eat so
much that she turned into a bloated, shapeless mass?
What made a well-to-do, young man turn
into an American Fascist . . . how did a brilliant
scientist come to believe that he actually
belonged on another planet?

In this revealing and unforgettable book, a
famous psychoanalyst tells you what went on
behind the doors of his private office, as
he tried to unravel the twisted emotions of
five men and women.

DON'T MISS

The Fifty-Minute Hour

A Collection of True, Psychoanalytic Tales

By ROBERT LINDNER

A Bantam Book At Your Newsstand Now

The Bestsellers Come From Bantam Books